2022

To my wonderful
Granddaughter- Ella

Love

Grandma Rjma

i

2019 Copyright Pending

NINA

by Dr. Zelma J. Frankhouser
Printed in the United States of America

ISBN: 9781980564249

Unless otherwise indicated, Bible quotations are taken from: The Thompson Chain-Referenced Bible, Fifth Improved Edition, King James Version. Copyright © 1988 by B.B. Kirkbride Bible Company, Inc. Indianapolis, Indiana, USA.

Cover

Designed By:
Dr. Zelma J. Frankhouser
2019

DEDICATION

Nina is dedicated to all the women who have been sexually abused, beaten, battered and separated from God. Their stories and suffering are dear to my heart and my lifetime goal is to let all women know, despite the types of lives they have lived, that God loves them and has a beautiful life for the one He calls His Beloved.

Even though this book is fiction, it epitomizes the lives of many women who find themselves not in control of their life. Their desire is to escape to be free of the pain they suffer. Sadly, too many run into the arms of Satan who showers them with his false promises.

Satan is the father of lies and his goal is to destroy all of God's beautiful creation. He will use our closest friends, family members and anything to blind us from the *Truth*. The *Truth* of God's Holy Word that brings us love, joy, peace, salvation and eternal life with Christ.

Please be part of defeating Satan and his evilness. I believe if each person leads one person to Christ, Satan will be totally defeated. Someone is waiting for you to take their hand to turn them around and lead them to the Cross so they will be able to stop running and start living a full and joyful life.

Zelma

THE MIRROR

I looked in the mirror, an image stared back;
One I did not know.
My heart became a fist..
It's ugliness strangled my chest;
My mind and soul.
I saw a face, one old, withered and worn;
I clenched my teeth.
My heart twisted.
The face looks back at me, then, laughs;
I do not know the beast.
I swallow in fear, then, I shake my fist;
Tell me, who is it I see?
My heart screamed.
The face glared, then, evilly it spoke;
It snarled, "It is thee".
I screamed in torment, I flailed and cried;
"Tell me, who speaks this lie."
My heart pounded.
The beast responded laced with vitric acid;
"Satan, your nemesis, yes, it is I".
I pled with God, this cannot be true;
"Remove this vision I see."
My heart sobbed.
I felt a hand lift me, a light appeared;
God was standing next to me.
My heart calmed.
He spoke, softly and lovingly;
My fear and anguish retreated.
My heart unlocked.
He said he loves me. I am his child;
Humbled I fell to His feet.
He declared His love for me;
"You are my child, the one I love."
He held me close, my pain vanished;
I stood amazed, no longer afraid.

Zelma

FOREWORD

The Other Side of the Cross Series

All books in the series, *The Other Side of the Cross* are fiction. All characters, towns and incidents are fictional. All incidents are products of my imagination. My books are a tapestry of my thoughts led by the Holy Spirit. They are written as a witness to the Glory of God and His desire that everyone can be part of His family and can have everlasting life in His Kingdom.

"Unto thee, O LORD, do I lift up my soul.
O my God, I trust in thee: let me not be ashamed, let not mine enemies triumph over me.
Yea, let none that wait on thee be ashamed: let them be ashamed which transgress without cause.
Shew me thy ways, O LORD; teach me thy paths.
Lead me in thy truth, and teach me: for thou art the God of my salvation; on thee do I wait all the day.
Remember, O LORD, thy tender mercies and thy loving-kindness; for they have been ever of old."
(Psalm 25:1-6 KJV)

SPECIAL THANKS

Without Christ and my family, this book would not be possible. To my husband, Bill, and my three children who supported me through my desire to complete my education, I cannot express in words how grateful I am for each of you.

Special thanks are given to my ten grandchildren and three great-granddaughters who keep me young and interested in learning and doing new things. Their love and encouragement bring immeasurable happiness to my senior years.

TABLE OF CONTENTS

"But if thine eye be evil, thy whole body shall be full of darkness. If therefore the light that is in thee be darkness, how great is that darkness!"
Matthew 6: 23 (KJV)

NINA

My name is Carolina, but everyone calls me Nina (rhymes with China). This is my story. I lived it. I hated it. I ran from it. I hid from it. I lied about it and God forgave me of it. That's just about the whole story. If you want the details, then read on and don't get embarrassed or shocked by what you read. The words you are reading are mine and I am ready to tell the truth. You see, I got tired of living it, hating it, running from it and hiding from it. I gave up and gave it to God since He is the only one big enough and strong enough to fix it and because God loved me in spite of my sinful life.

The end of my story is quite beautiful, in spite of the harsh beginning. It is really a love story when my real life began with a single transformative event – a miraculous heavenly intervention.

———————

"For thou [art] not a God that hath pleasure in wickedness: neither shall evil dwell with thee."
(Psalm 5:4 KJV)

Chapter 1

Tapestry

If my life story were a tapestry, a large oak tree would be woven in the middle with branches, long and sinewy, stretched out over the rough-brown fabric. The branches would be dotted with leaves of odd shapes and colors. Each leaf would represent different stages of my life. Some would shine with a rich-emerald luster, a symbol of amazing gifts of love, dearly and tenderly given to me. Others would be withered, dry and brittle and would fall and decay to be blown away and returned to dust. Those leaves would be a symbol of my past sins that were forgiven by my first love, Jesus.

Sometimes we look for that one special love for almost our entire life. The search begins at a serious pace as young women. We devote much of our time fantasizing about the one person who would fulfill our longing for true love and intimacy. Unfortunately, we can overlook the one who truly loves us and who waits for us and longs for us, sometimes for many years. That is pretty much how I wasted much of my younger years; little did I know that my true love was always beside me. He stood beside me during dark, terrible days and nights and cried with me when I was in pain and alone. He patiently waited until I was finally able to open my eyes and see the one who loves me more than his own life. At that time, my previous life that was torn with fear and pain dramatically changed. I could never have predicted the wondrousness of what was to come.

My first love was a love that began before I was born. It was a heavenly love offered to me by a man who lived over two-thousand years ago, Jesus. I cannot express in words the deep and satisfying feeling of joy that filled my being with hope and peace when I accepted his gift of love. Later in life, when I was in the autumn of my years, another incredible man entered my life. His name was Homer and his love completed my being; one that I thought I would never experience. He was an unexpected gift from God.

Homer was a godly and gentle man. He often blessed me with love words from the Bible. They were words, foreign to my ears, words of love and passion. Once, when I was terribly worried and afraid, Homer whispered as he held me in his arms, "O my dove, that art in the clefts of the rock, in the secret places of the stairs, let me see thy countenance, let me hear thy voice; for sweet is thy voice, and thy countenance is comely. Thy lips are like a thread of scarlet, and thy speech is comely: thy temples are like a piece of a pomegranate within thy locks." It was from the Song of Solomon and my Homer carefully chose them to confirm that his love for me was deep, faithful and enduring. The tapestry holds the complete story of my life and I want to share it with you.

The weaving of my life's tapestry begins in the swampy deep-south then moves to a desert valley about 100 miles inland of California's coastline. The final stitches display a grove of trees, richly-green and resplendent with evergreen fragrance. The redolence of their perfume flows from the tapestry and fills the air with a heavenly scent. Although the tapestry begins almost one hundred years before I was born in the swamps of the Deep South.

The Beginning

It was place with rarely-traveled dirt trails that connected it to outlying areas where hardy individuals settled what would become small towns and cities. It was a place where a few peaceful native Indians settled in the adjoining foothills. It was called Telegraph Trail and the only other residents were a husband and wife and a strange, smelly and dangerously evil ranch hand. The three of them scratched out a living as they ran a rest stop for occasional dusty stagecoach patrons and a lone-pony express rider. It was where evil lived and danger lurked within its boundaries, the Pony Express Trail.

From 1860 to 1862 it was the route of the pony express rider and stagecoaches that were often the target of bandits and criminals. Around the mid-1860s, telegraph poles were built along the Pony Express Trail and thus the name Telegraph Trail emerged. As time passed, wider and more frequently traveled dirt roads appeared as settlers followed the telegraph lines to distant unsettled regions of California. In time, homes were built and small towns dotted the barren countryside. Eventually cars replaced horses and horse-drawn carriages and the dirt roads were covered with blacktop. Around that time a new name emerged for the trail – Old Telegraph Road.

By 1960, the few remaining telegraph poles were removed; most had rotted and fallen down. There were also old railroad tracks that ran parallel to Old Telegraph Road. They were built to bring supplies and more people to the new towns. During the 1960s, they were buried under dirt then replaced with new ones a few miles away. The new railroad was used to move local farm produce to the main highway that ran through the long California Central Valley. No longer used as a main route for travel, Old Telegraph Road was vacant except for the sound of a few, noisy farm trucks.

During the 1860s, there were two buildings on the far west of Old Telegraph Trail; both were sod houses (adobe) with roofs made of mud and timber. The roofs were slanted to drain the annual meager rainfall into rain barrels. Another water source was a wild stream that flowed from the foothills about one-mile north of the adobe houses. The local Indians lived near it and stayed there year round. Water also flowed into underground streams and provided a good source for the three people who lived in the sod houses. It was their only source of fresh water and was much more convenient than hauling water from the wild stream and avoided the potential of trespassing through the Indians' camp.

Due to the dry climate, the surrounding area was mostly barren and didn't support a lot of wild game. The hot summer months stunted what few plants grew in the area. The landscape was covered with wild grasses, sagebrush and a few scraggly trees. Larger game in search of better food migrated to the higher mountains in the summer to feed and raise their young. The lack of lush vegetation and stately trees made the area appear desolate and unfriendly. In spite of the challenge of the local climate, one tree stood tall and strong. It was a strong oak tree.

It could be seen for miles. It displayed a thick trunk that was topped with a canopy of dense branches that spread out like gnarled scrawny arms. It was a landmark that was used to help pony express riders and stagecoach drivers see that they were headed in the right direction. It had other purposes too, which this book describes in later chapters. Over the years, it endured droughts, violent wind storms, lightning strikes and other potentially deadly wounds. Its deep roots and thick trunk kept it standing in spite of numerous injuries it endured. It was also the hanging tree for the few bandits who robbed the settlers and train. The hangman was the ranch hand who took much delight in his job.

As the ranch hand went about his work of changing tired horses for fresh, he could hear the complaints of the passengers who found his body odor to be overwhelmingly putrid. Over the years, he developed a vitriol hatred for them and all people in general. The horses were his only friends.

His hatred of people made him the perfect hangman. If a bandit was wounded or captured by one of the stagecoach drivers, he was brought to the rest stop. The testimony of the witnesses was good enough to get the bandit sentenced to death. Once everything was written down, signed, dated and all legal-like for the traveling lawman, the criminal was hung forthwith. When declared dead, the bandit was cut down and buried by the ranch hand in the land surrounding the adobe houses. As the years passed, the stagecoaches stopped coming and the adobe houses were abandoned and what happened at the rest stop was soon forgotten, as well as the graves.

During the 1940s, a farmer accidentally discovered those long-lost gravesites. He had been planting an almond orchard on the property contiguous to Old Telegraph Road. While digging, several full skeletons were uncovered. Not wanting to get in trouble with the law, digging was stopped and the skeletons were re-buried. To be safe, he moved his orchard several miles away. It was rumored that because the farmer abused the ghosts of the dead on the property, he suffered a terrible death. He came down with cancer. The town gossip was that he intentionally flew his plane into the side of a mountain. It exploded on impact and his body was burned so badly it was melted into the frame of the plane. The rescuers cut out the area of the cockpit that contained his seared body and buried it in the ground on his property. He would not be the only person whose badly-burned body couldn't be recovered from a fiery wreck.

During the 1950s and 1960s, local teens discovered Old Telegraph Road to be a great place to party and release their energy and live-out youthful romantic adventures. Sometimes, when there was a full moon, a few brave kids would hang out at the old adobe rest stop. They were known to bring their girlfriends or loose-women to their late-night parties. To make the night more interesting, the boys often had a plan to scare the girls. There were old tall-tales about the rest stop and teen boys used it to their advantage. It was said that when there was a full moon, the ghosts of the ranch hand and the bandits would climb out of their graves to haunt intruders.

Close to the midnight hour, a hidden teen would sneak up on the adobe house, kick the door and howl like a ghost. This would send the girls into a panic and the boys loved it. The boys would laugh and grab the scared girls. This led to lots of kissing by the boys to calm the girls. Almost always, the teen girls would slap the boys

10

when they got fresh and demand to be taken home. The old oak tree stood as a silent witness to these events, and some that were deadly and fed by roaring fires that could be seen for many miles. One evening, when Nina was present at one of the parties, the old oak tree would become the noble sentinel that protected the town from great harm. Nina's story records that event.

The time for the Old Oak Tree to protect the town people is soon to arrive.

*"Even so every good tree bringeth
forth good fruit;
but a corrupt tree bringeth
forth evil fruit."*
(Matthew 7:17, KJV)

Chapter 2

The Old Oak Tree

The old oak tree, gnarled and barren of leaves, stood alone on the side of Old Telegraph Road. It grew next to a two-lane road, primarily used by local farmers, about five or six miles from a small farming town. To the east of the road was nothing but foothills. For two or more miles the area was isolated and wild. Due to its isolation, it was a favorite hang-out for local teens. It was perfect for local high school kids to congregate at after Friday night games or for Saturday night parties. The area was safe from prying eyes and blabbermouths that delighted in spreading gossip about what happened on Old Telegraph Road.

Local hormone-driven high school males often brought dates to the area; some took dates labeled as loose women. Those women offered them more than teenage necking. Folks in town knew who they were and what they did. When the guys were with the town tramps, they got what they wanted and the women made a little extra money to supplement their measly income. They were often in their twenties or thirties and not hard on the eye. Most worked in town as waitresses, five-and-dime store clerks or

13

domestic help. Some took late-night shifts at the local bakery and food-packing plant.

It was common knowledge that dating the local loose women was safe. They were known not to kiss and tell. All were over jail-bate age and chances of them getting pregnant or sharing an embarrassing disease was slim. This was because the local doctor made certain they were free of sexually transmitted diseases such as syphilis. He was a soft-hearted and kind man. He doled out the new 1960 birth-control pill and other types of birth control prevention. It was his practice to regularly examine them for sexually transmitted diseases or unexpected pregnancies. In the event of a pregnancy, he was the person who helped families in the neighboring city find healthy, adoptable babies. He did this because he had delivered most of the younger town folks. He felt it was his duty to protect the young men from their sinful ways.

I, Nina, was one of those loose women. I did exactly as the others; I kept my mouth shut and met my regular appointments with the doctor. Yes, I was one because I didn't have a decent education. I had to make a living anyway I could. I was raised in the deep-south swamps. I didn't attend high school or much of any school. My family was dysfunctional; that is a nice way to say I was terribly abused as a child. My early home life was abysmal. To escape the constant sexual abuse from my older brothers, I ran away from home when I was sixteen. I lived on the streets, until I met Ornella.

My years on the streets made me strong and resilient. I survived by using my pretty face and shapely body to live. It wasn't easy living on the streets. I went hungry most of the time and almost froze to death during frigid winter nights. Then, one cold and dark night, I was beaten, robbed and raped. After that, I decided it was time to leave. Knowing my precarious lifestyle, I had wisely stashed some money in a broken fence post. After being attacked, I pulled it out and bought a bus pass and got a map. I looked for the farthest place to go. So, I decided to head west. I ended up in a small town in California's central valley; the small town west of Old Telegraph Road.

I clearly remember my first view of the valley. I was sitting on the first row of seats, right behind the bus driver. As the bus drove down the mountain pass, I saw a big valley with beautiful patches of green. It looked like heaven to me. The sun was shining, the hills were green and covered in purple and gold wild flowers. I could feel the warmth of the sun and I liked it.

15

My immediate thought was this was a place where I wouldn't freeze during winter. I knew I had made a good decision. For once, there were plenty of miles between me and my evil brothers; I thought they would never find me. Finally, I could exhale and relax.

As soon as I got off the bus I went to the local post office. On the bulletin board, I found an advertisement for a room to rent. It read, "Room to let. Females only. No kids, no pets and needs a job. Rent is reasonable. Call Fulton 3045. Ask for Ornella." I found the nearest pay phone and called. A woman about my age answered. She and I hit it off, right away. I told her I was running from a bad family and had been living on the streets. She didn't hesitate to agree to meet with me. She said she was a woman just like me and she wanted to help me. Not only did she rent a room to me, she found me two part-time jobs. She also taught me the ropes about being a tramp in the small town.

Ornella's life wasn't as bad as mine because her mother helped her. Ornella taught me my place and how to keep my distance from the other women; especially the respectable women. She made it clear that it was important to never flirt with their husbands or any man while working or when I accidentally saw them. I took her wise advice and followed it without question. This was a new start for me; I didn't want to fail.

The two of us shared the small house her mother owned. It was outside of town; not too far out and not too close. We were close enough to walk to work and far enough out not to be noticed. I discovered it didn't take long for the teen boys and adult males to find out who I was and what I did. Sadly, I wasn't ashamed of how I made my extra money.

Soon, I narrowed my clients to just a few adult males and an occasional teen. They never talked to me when I was waiting tables and never came to our house. All communication was done through my bosses. It was good business for them to have good-looking women waiting tables, and one who didn't object to providing extra services to their customers. This business practice kept their customers coming on a regular basis. It also gave me extra money for rent, plenty of food, and nice clothes to keep me attractive to clients.

For those first years, everything in my life went well. Within no time, I was in my mid-twenties and still very pretty. Then, one night on Old Telegraph Road my life took a sudden and tragic turn. The old oak tree was there as a witness to my terrible tragedy. You see, that night, there was a deadly accident that covered the old oak tree in blood. It was a Saturday night, lit with a full moon. It was when local teens gathered to drag-race on Old Telegraph Road.

Too Fast for the Road

Saturday night was when teens who thought they had the fastest cars met to hold a race-off against teens from the city. There was always a big crowd. Everybody dressed in the fashion of the times. The girls wore form-fitting sweaters and hip-hugging skirts or full skirts with crinoline slips. The guys wore tight pants; some wore white denim. Most wore dark-blue jeans just like the movie stars in the B-rated movies shown at the town's lone drive-in movie theater. Their shirts were starched and ironed with button-down collars. Shirts were tucked in and pants were held up with thin-black leather belts.

Most were drinking hard liquor or beer. One teen brought a bottle of Irish Mint and Irish Sloe Gin he had lifted from his dad's bar. He poured small amounts in some of the cokes the girls were drinking. Almost all were drunk or well on their way. The crowd was unruly and loud and the guys bragged too much and were rowdy. It could have been a scene from a 1960 B-rated movie. The girls flirted and teased their dates and were dressed in their sexiest clothes. Most parents carefully inspected their daughters' clothes before they left. It was common to sneak out with their tight clothes crammed in their purses.

Each night, the air was a mixture of spice, sweet perfumes and dense cigarette smoke, all heavily laden with potential danger. When the girls joined their group of friends, the air became heavy with a variety of perfumes and hairspray. It mingled with the greasy men's hair tonic and pungent after-shave cologne. Added to the intoxicating air was acrid cigarette smoke and cheap booze. The guys proudly displayed rockabilly hairstyles greased with Pomade[i] hair tonic.

It was an uncontrollable environment that led to male teens engaging in fist fights and overall teenage bedlam. That night was a repeat of similar nights. It was pierced with girlish screams as they pulled and clawed to separate the drunken combatants. Usually, the girls gave up, hugged each other and cried. Their black mascara and blue eyeshadow ran down their faces; they looked like crying clowns. Since the males were thoroughly inebriated with cheap liquor, their blows did little harm. Most attempts to hit their opponent ended with a fall. After they fell, the crowd erupted with kids joking and laughing.

After they fell, it was common to see combatants staggering off holding their abdomens. When free of the crowd of onlookers, and safely within the surrounding orchards they wretched up the contents of their stomachs. If a teen vomited too soon, the crowd burst out in loud protest. The putrid smell filled the air and soon mixed with the other odors of the night. Loud objections could be heard as everyone complained about the stench. The sick teen was jeered when he returned to the raucous group of party-goers. Then, more pushing and shoving ensued between the males. That night, the mayhem was lit from a full moon and by several small bonfires.

After things calmed down, everyone danced; totally uninhibited from adult supervision as they worked off their youthful energy. Their bodies were sweaty and glistened under the full moon. Girls' flowing skirts twirled as couples danced to the enticing beat of the music that blared from car radios. The local disk jockey attempted to imitate Wolfman Jack[ii] as he announced the top ten Billboard hits. Fast paced, steady-beat rock 'n roll songs such as *Tossin' and Turnin'* by Bobby Lewis[iii]; *Runaround Sue* by Dion DiMucci[iv]; and *Mother-in-Law* by Ernie K-Doe[v] filled the countryside air.

The slower songs provided opportunity for close embraces as dancers kissed and swayed to the smooth and easy beat of the music. Songs such as *Take Good Care of My Baby* by Bobby Vee[vi]; *Will You Still Love Me Tomorrow* by the Shirelles[vii]; and *Blue Moon* by the Marcels[viii]. The slow dances abruptly ended when a blast from a bull-horn announced it was time to prepare for the big race. Dancers immediately broke apart and car radios were turned off. All attention was given to the main event of the evening.

The teen holding the bullhorn announced that it was time to clear the road and move cars to the crossroad. The challenge was to begin – a race off between two competitors. Everyone ran to their cars. As they turned on their engines to move their cars they raced the engines in a macho display of male fearlessness. The sound of roaring engines started an adrenaline rush that filled their young bodies with anticipation of the coming race. The expectation of a thrilling contest between two challengers was to begin. The winner would be given the honor of having the fastest and meanest car around.

Dust and gravel flew in the air as cars cleared Old Telegraph Road. Once parked a safe distance from the finish line, kids scrambled out of the cars to take their places. Some stood safely behind parked cars – mostly to continue drinking their illegally purchased or lifted alcohol. Some used the privacy to engage in deep kisses as the teen males groped their female-squeeze for the night. The bravest group faced Old Telegraph Road straight on.

It wasn't unusual to see this fearless group scramble to safety when an errant racer didn't stop in time. To date, no one had been seriously injured. All cars had always safely slid to a stop without slamming into the parked cars. Although, there were many close calls that resulted in minor injuries such bruises or scrapes from flying gravel and rocks. This night was to be different.

During the re-positioning of cars, the two contestants drove their cars to the opposite crossroads; almost one mile straight down from the drunken onlookers. Races were always one-quarter mile in length with a full one-quarter mile or more for safe stops. At the three-quarter-mile mark stood the old oak tree. Its thick trunk was twisted and knotted from disease and age. Very few leaves grew from the branches and one sturdy branch hung out over the road. A male teen lay flat on the branch as he held the checkered finish flag. Another was on the branch above him where he held a flash light. He was responsible for signaling the all-clear to starters standing in front of the racers. Within seconds, everyone was in place for the race.

When a race was held against a city dude, most likely the two opponents didn't know each other. This was the case that night; the two racers only met a few hours earlier. One car held two Mexican teens from the city. They were dressed in black with hair slicked back with one long braid down the back. The other car was driven by a local kid who thought his Chevrolet was the hottest car ever; although it had never been tested against anything except rebuilt-junked-out cars.

However, the Mexicans were driving a souped-up GTO that sounded like a jet engine while idling. It was deep purple, with purple and white tuck 'n roll from Mexico. It looked hot, it sounded hot, and it ran hot. It was a fierce racing machine and had never been beaten. It certainly didn't look good for our small town kid. Not one to chicken out; he stood his ground with false bravado and was ready to get the race started.

Both racers lined up when the front ends of both cars were declared even by the starters. Once all rules for the race were explained, the starter yelled for the opponents to rev-up their engines. From our vantage point, it sounded like two planes roaring. The starters looked intently at both drivers to observe if they were ready, then hurriedly stepped to the side and waived the green starter flag. Dust and gravel flew from the car wheels as the cars fishtailed as they slid to a start. Eventually, the drivers got control and the cars straightened out. The two opponents were headed toward the crowd in a blast of speed.

The purple GTO took the lead and never lost it. During the entire race, the Chevrolet lagged at least one car length. Just as the GTO got close to the old oak tree, the driver accelerated. The car became air born. Stunned, the onlookers stood in amazement. Then, it slammed into the base of the tree and blew up. The impact shook the ground all the way to the finish line. It sounded like a bomb exploded. Pieces of tree, car and human body parts flew through the air. The acrid smell of smoke, gasoline and burning flesh consumed the air. Onlookers ran from the ghastly scene.

As they ran in a full-blown panic, all were gasping and choking as they tried to get free of the onslaught of deadly debris. Something small hit me square in the chest and stuck to my cotton blouse. It felt like a knife cutting deep into my breastbone. I screamed from the pain and shock of the impact. For some strange reason, I didn't immediately look to see what hit me. I turned my attention to what was happening around me. I saw other kids yelling as they panicked. They were running away or ducking under their cars. The cars seemed to be covered with shiny pools of liquid and steaming gasoline. Then, I turned my attention to my aching chest. I looked down at my blouse and grabbed something gruesome. It was a bloody, severed finger with a class ring on it. I fainted and fell to the pavement.

Two Days Later

I awoke two days later with a splitting headache. My fall resulted in a concussion and an enormous hematoma on my shoulder. Everything hurt and I couldn't raise my head or move my left arm. I tried to focus my eyes; but couldn't. I squeaked out a "Hello. Is anybody here?" Ornella ran in and immediately held me down. She ordered me to stay completely still and not to turn or lift my head. I started to cry and squirm only to discover I was tied to the bed. I tried to yell, but my lungs couldn't produce anything but a crackling sound. I began to slide into a panic attack. She yelled for someone to bring a shot. Within seconds, I saw a hypodermic needle pointed toward me. Someone swabbed my good arm with cotton dipped in alcohol; it was someone I didn't know.

Within seconds I felt the drug flood my body; it filled my mouth with a metallic taste. I asked for a glass of water. Ornella leaned over and gave me a drink of cool water. Then, my body went limp. I drifted off and slept. I dreamed about being at home with my mother. It was a good dream. We were sitting in our small aluminum fishing boat. I could feel its smooth movement over the swamp waters as mama paddled us along. It was a hot, humid day and the swamp was silent except for the call of a few wild birds. Mama turned to face me and smiled. She leaned close. With her hands she brushed the hair away from my face. I smiled back and laughed. It felt good to be with her. I felt safe and loved. Then I awoke. It was late into the night and our small house was dark. I began to panic again and this time I made a good, loud scream.

A strange woman flipped on the light and calmly walked to my bedside. She had been sitting in a chair, very close to me. She leaned forward and I smelled hard liquor on her breath mixed with cigarette smoke. I choked from it and she flew her head back and laughed. Her laugh was ugly and reminded me of a witches' laugh. I squirmed and discovered I wasn't tied down. I tried to raise my right hand to cover my mouth, only to find it was heavily bandaged.

That didn't stop me from putting my hand over my mouth as I attempted to block out her fetid breath. She stopped laughing and looked at me with eyes, red from liquor and lack of sleep.

She said, "Nina. I think that's your name. I am your roommate's mama. Yes. She has a mama. I know she don't talk about me much; but she got one. I ain't much to look at anymore, but once I was pretty and young just like you two. Now, I am worn out from too many years of boozin' and wild livin'. You been mighty sick and injured. When the kids brought you home, my daughter called the doctor. He couldn't come, 'cause lots of other kids were hurt real bad like. Ornella called me right up and begged me to come."

She continued, "I work in the city. I do the cleaning in the city hospital. She told me how bad off you were, so I lifted some good stuff to help you sleep and some bandages, syringes and needles. I knew you would be needin' something to keep you still 'cause you had a head that was hurt bad. So, I been givin' you Valium to keep you quiet until the swellin' in your head goes down."

So that was what was in the shot; and she was the person who gave me the shot. I relaxed and thanked her for helping me. She shared she didn't need any thanks; any friend of her daughters was family and she was ready to help her family in time of need. She asked me if I was hungry and I said, "Yes ma'am. I am really hungry and thirsty for something cold; like a real cold soda."

She smiled, left for a few minutes and returned with a bologna sandwich and a cold cola. That was the best meal I had ever eaten. I started to gobble it down, but she told me to take it slow because what I ate would come right back up. She said she didn't want to wash vomit off me; she couldn't stand the smell of vomit. I laughed, slowed my eating and kept the food down.

I asked her what day and time it was. She said I had been in bed almost two full days and was clear out of my head most of the time. That was why she tied me down. She said I could have really hurt myself from tossing and fighting and screaming like I did. She had been in hospitals long enough to know what to do when someone had a head injury. She had seen what happened to people who didn't and most died an awful, painful death or were not right in the head for the rest of their life.

I thanked her for taking good care of me. I knew that even though I found her cigarette and alcohol-laced breath repulsive, she had a good heart and meant me well. I asked her, "When can I get up or even sit up?" She said to wait until daylight when her daughter comes home from her night shift at the bakery. The local bakery crew worked nights so that bread, pastries, pies and cakes were fresh for the local restaurants and grocery stores. Ornella liked the job because she was out of sight of the nosy people in our small town. They enjoyed spreading gossip because they knew what she was and how she spent her weekends. We both understood our proper place was to stay out of sight, and we made sure to do just that.

Our jobs were always night or early morning jobs. At that time, I helped the prep-cook at a local diner and my shift ended by 5:00 a.m. when it opened for breakfast. I also had a part-time shift at a local bar as a cocktail waitress. That was where my boss secured my clients whom I met at motels in the city. It was always someplace located outside the city, about ten miles north of where I lived. The motels were a good distance from the city's central businesses. That was where the women, the respectable women, in our town travelled and shopped for the latest-style clothes and met friends for lunch.

Knowing the potential danger of being seen, I always conducted my business in secluded areas of the city. I didn't want to get the respectable town people mad. I wanted to stay there because I believed I was safe from mean brothers.

I had clients whom I trusted not to rough me up. They didn't beat me when they were drunk. Not like some of Ornella's clients. Sometimes she came home with black eyes and bruises. She never shared with me what happened; even though I asked her, many times. I knew who the men were. I didn't like them and I kept a good distance from them. As for me, I was fortunate that my clients treated me well. I could select my clients and I was able to say yes or no as I pleased. I was never pressured to be what I was; a prostitute.

My clients often told me that I conducted my business with class. It may have been because I chose to limit my drinking. I always wanted to be sober just in case I had to escape a bad situation. I thought that being in control of my senses assured my security and freedom. My freedom was being free of my brothers. My security was my two jobs that provided a roof over my head and no more living on the street.

Although deep inside my soul, I was ashamed. I knew I was sinning, but I didn't care because my life was better than what I endured as a child. I was sure that my new life, in this small town, was the best chance I would ever have for a good life. I was confident I was making the right choices. Most nights I was haunted by nightmares. Those nights I woke up screaming, drenched in sweat and terrified.

Oh how I needed Jesus and someone to help me find Him.

"The fear of man bringeth a snare: but whoso putteth his trust in the LORD shall be safe."
(Proverbs 29:25 KJV)

Chapter 3

Paralyzed in Fear

The years after the horrible wreck on Old Telegraph Road my mind was imprisoned in a constant state of fear. I couldn't clear it of what happened; the tragedy added to my ongoing anxiety that my brothers would find me. More often than usual, I was overcome in fear so terrible I would shake. As a result, I carried a debilitating affliction inside my soul of looming disaster. Almost every day I was drenched in gut-wrenching panic. I was bound and paralyzed by Satan who used my pain to separate me from God. It was easy for Satan because I was totally ignorant of God. The years after my mama died I lived in isolation and was enslaved by my evil brothers. I was living in darkness and Satan liked it that way.

The only knowledge I had of God was when my aunt found one of my brothers sexually assaulting me. Her response was to inform me about sin and hell. Since I was very young and unchurched, my immediate reaction was to run from God and from my family. I believed that if I ran from everyone and everything, I would gain complete freedom. Little did I know that running from God is a snare that Satan sets to trap and destroy God's children. As a result, for many years I was caught in Satan's trap. I had reacted to primal instinct and ran from my awful past.

When I fled from my wicked brothers, seeking God was not my immediate thought. In retrospect, it should have been my first thought. I fled until a great expanse of America separated me from them. During those years I was a prostitute and I put on a false bravado. I presented myself as courageous and clever. Instead, I was a coward; hiding, worrying, and incredibly fragile. I was a prisoner who was bound in Satan's grasp and polarized by his lies. I was literally drowning in sin because I believed Satan's lie that I was finally safe. Little did I know that I was not safe; Satan had his own plan for me.

I put my trust in Satan. He blinded me by convincing me I could control my life. The most deceitful of his lies was that it was my life to ruin. I was God-ignorant. I had no knowledge that God created all of Heaven, Earth and all living creatures. I relied upon myself for my safety. I didn't understand that God, who loves us because we are His children, was my true protector and my refuge. As a result, I failed in my shabby attempt to control my life. It took several years for me to discover how badly I botched up everything. Clearly, without question, I lived those years in total conflict with God as I ran from Him.

My running began when my mama died. I was very young when she died, about ten or eleven. My family lived in the deep south. Our home was well hidden in the swamp. We had no neighbors or immediate family members in our area and no church. Poppa liked the seclusion; he could hunt, fish, get drunk and live the life he wanted. We seldom had visitors, and when we did they were usually wild Cajun traders. Prior to mama's death, the Cajuns were a welcomed break in our secluded lifestyle.

Mama and poppa weren't Cajun; they weren't raised in the swamps. Since Cajuns were so different than us, I was mesmerized by their dissimilarity. Their rhythmic language sounded like someone singing and their carefree ways enchanted me. I found them to add a splash of color and variety to my family's reclusive lifestyle. Their occasional visits brought news of outlying areas that were unknown to me.

I would listen to them and try to imagine what the people and the towns looked like. Since I was born in the swamp and had little education, it was difficult for me clearly picture the outside world.

They also brought interesting things to trade with my poppa. He hunted and had pelts and skins of swamp critters to trade; especially alligator hides. The Cajuns brought a variety of goods to trade for the hides such as toys for me, tools and knives for poppa and my brothers, and pretty fabrics and new cooking utensils for mom.

After their business was concluded, the next day was spent telling tall tales as they drank a variety of homemade moonshine. By nightfall my brothers, poppa and the Cajuns were extremely drunk. In their inebriated condition, arm wrestling and fights broke out. During the men's rough games, mama would gather me in her arms. We would hide in one of our storage shacks; well locked and safe from their drunkenness.

The Dance of the Python

There was one time when a Cajun secretly followed mama and me to the storage shack. He was drunk and bent on finding a woman for lovemaking. He climbed through a side window of the storage shack. He grabbed mama and tried to kiss and fondle her. She couldn't scream because he had his hand tightly pressed over her mouth. My survival instincts took over and I hid behind some sacks. As I secretly peered around the sacks, I saw mama struggle. I gathered my little-girl courage and ran for help. I escaped through the open window the Cajun used. I ran to poppa and screamed that a bad man was hurting mama in the storage shack. Poppa told me to get in the house and stay there, no matter what happened. I ran to the house and hid under my bed. From my hiding place, I heard screams, loud banging noises and then more yelling. Then, nothing but silence. I began to cry and shake from fear of the unknown.

In a few minutes, that seemed like hours, I heard poppa's heavy footsteps on the porch and then a loud thump as he kicked open the door. He was sobbing and moaning. I crawled from under my bed and peered to see something horrifying. He was holding mama in his arms. Her body was limp and she was smeared with bright red blood. I screamed and ran to her. I don't remember much of anything else except that I bolted. I ran out the door trying to escape the awful sight of my momma slowly dying in poppa's arms.

I ran and ran. I scrambled through tall dry grasses, jumped over dead tree limbs, and climbed into a tree, gnarled from disease. To steady myself, I grabbed what I thought was a tree branch. The branch began to slowly move and twist. It wound around my tiny arm. I looked at my arm and dead into the eyes of a python. I screamed and struggled to get free. The python's strong muscles flexed and tightened. The more I struggled, the tighter it gripped me. I couldn't free myself so I screamed for help.

Immediately, I heard heavy boots running through the swamp brush. I turned to look and my brothers were headed toward me; one had a large machete and the other had an alligator-skinning knife. Within seconds they climbed up the tree and cut me free of the deadly python. I collapsed in the arms of my oldest brother. I felt safe, but then, I looked into his eyes. They were red from moonshine and his face was heinously contorted. I could smell his breath; it was rancid with moonshine.

His face was twisted and distorted I gasped in surprise. He began to laugh and it sent a chilling shudder through my entire body. Not knowing how to respond, I raised my arms for him to comfort me. He laughed again. This time it was dripping with evil. I started to shake because innately I knew it meant imminent danger. I began to panic and I tried to free myself but his arms were too strong. He turned to face my other brother and threw me into his arms. The two of them jostled me back and forth as if I was a toy. They were full of hard liquor and unable to control their actions or understand they were hurting me.

I begged them to put me down; I wanted to go to mama. My pleading brought on more rough housing and eventually one of my brother's dropped me. I was exhausted and my arms and legs were useless. I couldn't pull myself up. I tried to crawl away. They laughed at my futile attempt to escape. They began to dance in a lurid, menacing fury. I can still vividly recall watching them. I knew something terrible was going to happen to me.

Seeing I had no way to escape, in an attempt to protect myself, I folded into a fetal position. I lay on the dirt and dry grass fearing for my life. Then, one of my brothers lifted me and held me up in his arms as he danced wildly in circles; similar to a pagan ritual. I vomited and urinated on him. He threw me down in disgust and kneeled close to me. In his drunkenness he sneered, "I will finally get even with you. You ain't no special thing. We know how mama favors you. Now it's time to show you who is your master."

I gasped, then spit in his face. He hit me across the mouth so hard I think I lost consciousness for a few seconds. When I opened my eyes, I lay on the ground in fear. I was paralyzed waiting for what would next happen. Then, he lay over me and his weight prevented me from struggling. All I remember was a burning pain between my legs and screaming for mama. For the second time I lost consciousness. I lay unknowing of what was happening to me. All this happened as mama died that night in the arms of my poppa. She died from knife wounds inflicted accidentally by my poppa as he wrestled with the Cajun.

I have no memory of how or when I was taken back to our house. I vaguely remember lying in my bed floating in and out of consciousness; screaming in terror if anyone came close to me. My next clear memory was standing at mama's grave, softly whimpering from emptiness and fear of living without her. Not only had I lost my mama, but my brothers were now my enemy and tormentors. After her death, they became more brazen with their attacks on me. They became incredibly wicked.

It seemed as if their only desire was to be evil and destructive. They sought to murder and destroy anything and everyone within their path.

Poppa couldn't control them. He was no good after mama died. He took to drinking and never again went hunting, fishing or trapping and skinning alligators. Poppa took up sitting on the front porch with his liquor for his companion. He was totally unaware of the incredible wickedness that had taken control of his home. As for me, I was forgotten and I became a prisoner in my own home. I was an innocent victim, tormented and abused and praying for a way to escape.

Eventually, I stopped crying. My heart became as hard as my life. My chest always felt as if it was tight, like a fist. My only hope was my plan to escape. Instinctively I knew I would need good survival skills. To prepare myself for my escape, I taught myself to cook, clean and to how to handle a knife and rifle. I decided it was best to learn those things so I would be prepared to survive on my own. The years after mama died, I didn't go to school; my education stopped at fifth grade.

In time, I grew out of the dresses my mama sewed for me. I wore my brother's clothes; the clothes they wore when they abused me. I would wash them until I thought their meanness was gone. How I hated wearing their clothes. At first they were too big; but the hard work I did helped me grow and they began to fit. I grew tall and

41

had strong hands, arms and legs. My hair was never cut; I wore it tightly pulled into a pony tail to keep it off my sweaty face. I could cut and carry wood and could shoot a gun or rifle as good as my brothers. I also learned to distinguish snakes from tree branches. I killed any snake I saw and those that were edible, I cooked for my family. I also learned not to fight my brothers when they raped me; if I fought, they beat me. My life was a living hell and I never stopped searching for a way to escape. Those years hardened me and prepared me to live on the streets.

Waiting to Strike

Even though I seemed to be in control of my life at home in the swamp, my life was a contradiction to what was going on inside of me. Every thought, breath and action I took was the result of gut-wrenching terror. I can only compare how I felt by comparing it to a tornado. My tornado began as a menacing cloud that hovered over me when mama died. When things were calm, the ugly cloud stayed in the sky, watching me.

Then, when the cloud flattened; it resembled a demon with three large horns. I knew that it would soon release its tremendous power to inflict pain and destruction. In it I saw the death of my mama and abuse by my three brothers. As I watched it I could see my life swirl around in it. Then when it birthed its powerful, destructive funnel cloud I knew my brothers were on the prowl. I tried to run from it because it was my brothers chasing me to inflict their vicious hate on me.

As I ran, it would wind and slink like a snake seeking its prey. It gathered more power as it rapidly sped forward to strike. Before it lurched to strike it would pause and sneer at its victim. I was the victim and my brothers were the funnel cloud. Once perfectly positioned, they would attack with rapid and deadly precision. I would fight to break free. My attempts were always futile. My young body and broken soul was sucked up into their evilness and tortured.

When finished, my body was spit out, ripped and bloody. They cast me to the earth. My screams for help were useless; they fell on the vast silence of the swamp. After each attack, I heard their evil laughs as they retreated. What I didn't know was that it was Satan laughing. He had completed his mission; one more of God's precious children were being destroyed. Pleased with his conquest, Satan rapidly ascended into his monstrous black cloud that watched and waited for a chance to torture me. As I lay broken after each rape, I cursed God. This pleased Satan.

When I finally escaped and lived on the streets, the funnel cloud still hovered over me. I always knew it was watching. That is why I ran but couldn't escape. It always knew where I was. When I lived with Ornella, I tried to eradicate my fears with my new friend; valium and other drugs. I sought their soothing comfort that gave me sleep and temporary relief. For many years, I ran toward them and welcomed them with passionate surrender. They became my master and God and my best friends. I didn't object because they were Ornella and her mother's friends, too.

Tragic Loss

Rosalinda, Ornella's mother also introduced me to opioids and other street narcotics. They both were addicted to them. They didn't hesitate to share their poison with me and I didn't refuse. For the first few years, I used them occasionally. I never used them with clients or during work; only when I desperately needed to sleep and escape my night terrors. As for Ornella, I discovered she shared them with her clients. That was the reason she often came home with bruises. One Sunday night, she staggered into our house almost dead from an overdose. She was pale and her clothes were stained from vomit, blood and urine. Rosalinda sent for the local doctor. He immediately responded and came to our house. He wasn't one to be afraid to be seen in our neighborhood. He often made house calls to those of us who lived on the outskirts of town. He believed it was his duty to take care of us. If we were well, then he thought he was protecting the good people in the town.

In our small neighborhood were other people who were labeled as outcasts. They were residents who were not quite right in the head; men, women and children. They lived together in small-shanty houses a few blocks from my house. Most walked the streets at night, talking to themselves and peering in shop windows. They were harmless. They could be seen going through garbage cans collecting all sorts of trash. They were people who had the misfortune of being different. Some were intelligent and some weren't. None were known to be friendly; they were almost all recluses who preferred to be left alone.

From their night prowls, they carried items they found to their homes; their treasures. Their homes attested to their nighttime thefts; all types of cast off and broken items littered their lawns.

On occasion, in the very early mornings, business owners found one of them asleep on the sidewalk. They would call local police who would take them home. Sadly, a business owner or passerby would stumble upon one who died on the streets during their nightly treasure hunt. They were buried in unmarked graves in the town cemetery. They lived and died what normal folks called a wretched life.

As for Ornella, Rosalinda and me, we weren't much different than they. We lived a reclusive life and used the night to hide our sins. The night Ornella stumbled home close to death could have ended differently. A business owner could have found her as she lay on the streets, dead from her addiction. The three of us were just a few steps away from the outcasts. We didn't think so; but we were.

The night she came home almost dead from an overdose, I began to realize the sadness of our life. It didn't stop me from seeking the potions that gave me temporary peace and drug-induced sleep. As for Ornella, she recovered only to continue her death spiral as she lived trapped inside Satan's funnel cloud. Soon, he would have one more conquest of which to boast.

Ornella was addicted to heroin. She said that nothing else could give her the wonderful feeling she got from shooting up heroin. To secure it she walked the streets of the city located almost ten miles north of our small town, the same place I hid to conduct my sinful business with clients. Buying heroin on the street was dangerous and sometimes deadly. It was on those streets that she was beaten and thrown aside.

Those who sold her heroin often followed her and took her jewelry, money and then the heroin they sold her. Each time she made a purchase, she knew she was in danger; but her craving for it was stronger than her common sense. Once after she was robbed by her supplier, she tried to hustle clients on the street to get money to make another buy. The city cops picked her up and jailed her.

During her jail sentence she couldn't get heroin. Her addictive brain screamed for the drug and her body fell into dope sickness. She almost died from constant vomiting and diarrhea. In her dehydrated state, she collapsed on the jail floor. The police found her semi-conscious and writhing from hallucinations. Wisely, they transferred her to the county hospital for medical treatment. It was there she spent the rest of her jail sentence.

While in the hospital, Rosalinda and I visited her. Our hearts were ripped from us as we watched her spiral down into Satan's abyss. She was incredibly thin, pale and often disoriented. We didn't know how to pray or even thought about asking God for help. We waited, worried and continued with our own destructive lifestyle. As the time passed, during our visits, she seemed to climb out of her stupor. Eventually, she came around and was ready to be released. Once home with us, we encouraged her to keep clean; but deep inside we knew she couldn't do it. Not with both of us doing drugs.

A few weeks after she was released, she started back working at her old jobs. She also reconnected with her previous clients. Rosalinda and I pushed our fears aside as it appeared her recovery was successful. Things returned to normal. Then, one cold winter night Ornella was very late coming home. Rosalinda was worried and paced the floor. As she waited, she heard a car door slam and then skid off as if to escape before anyone saw it. She ran out the front door and saw her daughter sprawled in the street. She screamed for me to help her.

I had been lightly sleeping because I, too, was worried about Ornella. I had heard the driver's tires squeal as he drove off. I instinctively knew something bad happened. I jumped out of bed and ran into the cold night air. Shivering, I saw Rosalinda kneeling on the pavement holding Ornella in her arms. She was wailing and rocking back and forth. Ornella's face was ashen white and frozen in a horrifying expression. Her mouth was gaping open and her eyes were wide as if she had witnessed something gruesome. She was dead and appeared to have been dead for quite a while.

I kneeled by Rosalinda and tried to close Ornella's eyes. They were fixed in a ghastly stare. A cold chill ran down my spine. I strained to help Rosalinda lift her so we could carry her into the house. To balance myself I wrapped my arm behind her back and my hand felt a rather large hole that was full of sticky-dried blood. I immediately knew she must have died several hours before she was thrown from the car and that the gaping hole was the cause.

I winced, but didn't say anything to Rosalinda. I leaned over and told her, "Let's get her in the house. Our creepy neighbors are standing in the street, looking at us." That stopped her screaming and she seemed to come to her senses. Her beautiful daughter was dead and no amount of crying and sobbing could ease her pain. As best we could, we carried her into the house.

She wasn't limp; her body had stiffened and it was incredibly difficult getting her through the front door. I was beginning to think we couldn't do it, but somehow we did. I began to get nauseous; I was covered in black sticky blood and Ornella smelled of death. As soon as we got her inside I rushed to cleanse myself of the stench. I ran to the bathroom and lost the contents of my stomach. I wretched until there was nothing left. I stood and looked at myself in the mirror, I was covered in dark-dried blood. I tore off my pajamas. I threw them on the floor and decided to burn them. I knew the sight of them, even if I could wash them clean, would be too much for me.

After I showered and put on clean clothes, I dropped my soiled pajamas into a paper bag. I ran outside and threw them into the trash can. I decided to burn them. As they burned I decided to quit drugs and stop my sinful life. I vowed I was going to start over, even if I had to escape to a new town. That was what I could do. Yes, run. I was used to running. It was my only escape from Satan's funnel cloud that was always watching and chasing me. I finally realized my life was a mess and it could have been me that was dumped in the street. I believed I would be next; after all, Satan wasn't satisfied with just Ornella, he wanted me, too.

Ornella was buried in our town cemetery, close to the unmarked graves. It was a cold and gloomy day; dark clouds hovered over us. I looked up and a cold-eerie shudder of impending doom ran down my spine. Was the funnel cloud watching us? Was it happy that Ornella was dead and in the cold grave? Then my thoughts turned to Rosalinda and her pain of losing her daughter. My heart was saddened for Rosalinda as I looked at her mourning over the loss of her only child.

It wasn't much of a graveside service. Just Rosalinda, Ornella's bosses, the local doctor and a few of our crazy neighbors and me were there. The business owners she worked for took up a collection to pay for the funeral and a small headstone. Her name and birthdate and date of death were engraved on it. The words "Finally at Peace" were written above them. I cried along with the others.

The preacher for the small church located not far from us spoke a few words. He read a few verses in the Bible and said a short prayer. There was no music, no singing, and only one or two small bouquets of flowers. It began to softly rain after the ceremony; everyone left right away to avoid getting wet as they walked home. As Rosalinda and I walked, she said, "The valley fog is coming. It will be a dark and lonely winter. I dread the fog. It reminds me of death." I held her hand as we walked away in silence. My thoughts were focused on how I could break free of my addictions. I had no idea how to start or who to go to.

The person that would help me had been next to me for many years. God, in his infinite wisdom, knew exactly who I needed to help me and he prepared her for the task.

"For all the law is fulfilled in one word, even in this; Thou shalt love thy neighbour as thyself."
(Galatians 5:14 KJV)

Chapter 4

We Ain't Perfect

After Ornella's death, life for Rosalinda and me changed. For one, she started going to church. She asked me, many times to accompany her. I always refused. After all, God wasn't part of my life; I believed it was He who abandoned me and my mama. I was certain church wasn't and never would be part of my life. I didn't need that Jesus god-man and I didn't want anyone interfering in my life. I told Rosalinda that if she felt better going to church, praying and all that stuff, that was fine with me. As for me, I told her to leave well enough alone. I was doing just fine.

I didn't want to be part of those Bible-toting hypocrites. Yes, hypocrites. What made them think they were better than me? If they had walked in my shoes and gone through my dreadful life, they would know why I felt this way. For certain, not one of them could understand my pain and anguish. Nor could they walk in my shoes every day and survive as I had. Not one of them knew what it was like to live in fear, every day and every moment. No, not any were as strong as I; they couldn't handle the tragedies I had endured. I was tough enough to stay alive but not strong enough to conquer my inner fear. It controlled my every thought and action. I was a survivor and I believed I did it on my own. I was certain I didn't need to cry on the shoulder of a god who abandoned me.

I wasted many years running from my past. I depended upon drugs for my relief. My drugs were my lover and savior. They were what calmed my nerves and buried my thoughts of the hell I had endured. I loved them. I sought them. I sold my body and soul for them. We were partners in a love-dance, sadly it was a dance with unfaithful lovers. You see, Satan does that to people.

He gives them the sweetness of peace as he kills them with his venom. The poison he gave me was what I thought I needed to overcome my living hell. Satan knows we humans are easy targets; he knows us better than we know ourselves. That is why he was successful in the Garden of Eden. He knows our weakness and he preys upon it. He hovers over us just as the ominous-black clouds do; the ones pregnant with destruction and death.

The drugs helped for short periods of time. When the soothing effect of the drugs ended, I needed more. If I didn't get more, I found myself facing another painful day. It seemed as if I was always running and searching for safety. Running was what I believed would keep me safe from my brothers. I was convinced they could never find me because the miles between us were too many. I believed they were too ignorant to figure out how to search for me.

My security was the great expanse of country between us. I was wrong. I would discover how wrong I was; that was another of Satan's lies. My life was controlled by Satan's lies. He told me I wasn't worthy of love. I accepted his lie and believed no one could ever love me. After all, I was a sinful tramp. How could anyone love me, especially a perfect god.

Satan convinced me that Rosalinda's church friends were hypocrites. He told me my only true friend was myself. As a result of listening to Satan, I couldn't break free of my addiction. I continued my dance with the drugs; my lover and comforter. I tried to keep the love-dance controlled, but I failed. My intention was to take them infrequently but, my lover was demanding and never satisfied with an occasional love-dance.

In a short time my addiction took a tighter hold on me. Also my behavior changed. I was often late to work and when there, not fully cognizant of my actions. I felt as if I was in a dream and not fully aware of my surroundings. My thoughts were foggy and my speech was slurred. The people I worked with recognized the difference. Most of them thought it was because I was depressed from the loss of Ornella. I let them think it as they tried to comfort me. I couldn't break free; Satan's poison was in my system almost all the time. You see, I became the real hypocrite. I was the one living a lie.

Even Rosalinda tried to help me. Since she got involved with the church people, she was clean and sober. One day, she told me how it happened. "Nina. I got to tell you something wonderful. Last Thursday night at church meeting, I got freed of my taste for liquor and drugs. Can you believe it? It happened so fast I don't know what caused it?" I looked at her with suspicion. I thought she must be crazy. How can anyone break free of a lifetime of drinking and using street drugs? I answered in a mocking voice, "Sure. Sure, and I am a princess who lives in a castle." Immediately I saw that my nasty response hurt her. She put her head down and started to cry.

I instantly felt guilty. I said, "Oh Linnie (that is what I called her). I am sorry. I didn't mean to hurt you. You know how I feel about all that church stuff." She pensively replied, "Can I go on? Are you done with making fun of me? Ya' know, it ain't good to mock what God does. You could be in for a good whooping from Him." I chuckled, "I guess it won't be the first time he whooped me, and it won't be the last. I think am strong enough to take a whooping." She didn't laugh. Her demeanor became more serious. She answered in a firm voice, "You don't know what you are a sayin'. You are too ignorant. That's it. You are ignorant about God and how much He loves you."

My temper flared. I yelled, "Don't you ever, ever call me ignorant. It's not my fault I didn't get a good education and it's not my fault I didn't learn about God." Instead of getting angry, she did something strange. She moved toward me and put her arms around me. That was the very first time anyone hugged me other than my mama. At first I stiffened and tried to push her away. She was stronger than me. She tightly held me. I relaxed. It was good to have someone hold me the way she did. Oh, how I needed to be held and loved. I felt as if something moved from her to me in that hug. I can't explain it. It was the Holy Spirit loving on me.

We both began to cry. She said, "Let's sit down at the kitchen table. We need to talk a bit. You know, we never did talk much. Since we lost our beautiful Ornella, we have been nothing but strangers." My legs felts wobbly and she helped me to one of our unmatched, well-used chairs. None of our furnishings were new; we bought the furniture from the local second-hand store. The store owner rounded up furniture, appliances and such from all over; not just from our small town.

He and his wife cleaned and repaired it as best they could. Then they sold it in an old building that smelled like moth balls. I don't think they ever opened a window or door to let in fresh air. Whenever we bought something, we let it set outside in the sun for a full day to remove the awful odor. Sometimes the smell was still so strong that we turned fans on it and opened the windows. It wasn't the best furniture; but it was good enough for us.

We sat in the mismatched chairs at the silver and grey kitchen table. The top was smooth and looked like grey and white marble. I think it was a plastic-coated veneer. It was marked with a variety of stains and burns from cigarettes and hot pans. Even though it wasn't perfect, Linnie kept it clean. She tried to hide some of the stains with her home-made place mats that she crocheted. Since Ornella died, she had taken up crocheting and other crafts to keep her hands busy and her mind occupied. She also said it kept her from reaching for a hard drink or a cigarette. Since her sobriety, her body odor and foul breath had greatly improved. I was grateful for the change, it made being around her much more pleasant.

Not only had Linnie's physical appearance changed, her mannerisms were different. She didn't scowl as much and she laughed more. Linnie also began to listen to the radio and sing along with the songs. I discovered she had a pleasant voice that was soft and on key. I didn't mind her singing as long as it was popular tunes. One day she was singing church songs. She could tell I didn't like it. She said, "You don't like them church songs much. Do you?" I shook my head to show my dislike, then said, "Try to sing them when I'm not here." She shrugged and smiled and said, "Someday, I know you will sing them with me."

I ignored her comment and didn't get upset. I turned my back to her and smiled at her answer. She wasn't one to give up and I respected her strength and devotion to her faith. Even though we didn't see eye to eye about all her religious stuff. Of course, I didn't like her when I first saw her. She smelled bad and her voice reminded me of a witch. Lately, either she changed or I was just getting used to her voice and mannerisms. That day we were finally able to sit at the kitchen table and talk about Ornella.

Those talks felt good because we had begun to get along. Whatever the reason for my change of attitude, that first day we talked was when we became friends. During our visits, Linnie never preached to me; if she had, I would have walked away. That would have ended any future attempts from her to convince me to go to church. You see, I was wrapped in a thick layer of distrust and sin and wasn't ready to let anyone get too close.

Many times we talked about why the police didn't try to find who shot Ornella. I think the reason they didn't was because our local doctor told the police that she died of a drug overdose. There was no mention from the police or the doctor about the hole I felt in her back. I was irritated about it, but who would listen to what a drug-addicted prostitute had to say? In our town, no one. We were white trash who lived outside of town, an acceptable distance from the town's respectable people. We lived an existence that labeled us women of ill-repute. We were thought to be dirty and dumb undesirables that nice people whispered about. It was well known, that if good people got too close to us, our filth would rub off on them. So, they kept their distance.

Linnie and I had many talks about all these things. She told me it wasn't like that in church. Everyone was welcome, no matter how shameful or sinful they thought they were. After all, she said, "Christ loves everyone; even prostitutes, criminals, and the poor." When she shared that, I listened and didn't mock her. Church was the place where she felt normal and clean. She talked about a specific church service where she thought the preacher was talking to her. He spoke on Galatians, 5:14. She had a Bible setting on the table (that I always avoided). She opened it and read, "For all the law is fulfilled in one word, even in this; Thou shalt love thy neighbour as thyself."

She added, "The preacher said none of us can do this all the time. We ain't perfect and we make all kinds of mistakes. But the Bible says it clear, we need to love each other no matter if we is different and some of us is more different than others. That made real good sense to me. I hope it helps you like it did me." I didn't immediately answer. I tried to understand it. Since I knew nothing about the Bible, the verse was totally foreign to me. My only knowledge of the Bible was that sinners go to hell. The idea that loving each other even if we are different was new to me. I just didn't know how to respond when I heard the verse. My hesitation started Linnie reading again.

She read more of the same chapter in Galatians, starting at verse 15. "But if ye bite and devour one another, take heed that ye be not consumed one of another. This I say then, Walk in the Spirit, and ye shall not fulfil the lust of the flesh. For the flesh lusteth against the Spirit, and the Spirit against the flesh: and these are contrary the one to the other: so that ye cannot do the things that ye would. But if ye be led of the Spirit, ye are not under the law. Now the works of the flesh are manifest, which are these; Adultery, fornication, uncleanness, lasciviousness, idolatry, witchcraft, hatred, variance, emulations, wrath, strife, seditions, heresies, envying, murders, drunkenness, reveling, and such like: of the which I tell you before, as I have also told you in time past, that they which do such things shall not inherit the kingdom of God. But the fruit of the Spirit is love, joy, peace, longsuffering, gentleness, goodness, faith, meekness, temperance: against such there is no law. And they that are Christ's have crucified the flesh with the affections and lusts. If we live in the Spirit, let us also walk in the Spirit. Let us not be desirous of vain glory, provoking one another, envying one another."

When she finished, I was even more confused. I said, "Linnie, what does all of it mean? I understand the sinning part but a whole lot of it confuses me. I guess I got a heap of learning ahead of me if I want to understand the Bible." Linnie answered, "I am not real sure what it all means. I guess I need to ask the preacher to help me with it." I slowly got up and pushed the chair under the table. I said, "I got to get ready for work. Maybe we can talk about this another time." The real reason I walked away was because I saw myself in those words. I was living in sin and the fear of hell had started to rise up inside me. I needed to get away and find my friend, my drugs, for comfort.

Linnie was wise to what I was about to do. She followed me into my bedroom, stood in the doorway and said, "Let me pray for you. Please, you need the strength of the Holy Ghost to resist the temptation of the bottle you are reaching for." I turned my head sideways and gave her a malicious glare. She jumped back and said, "Satan. Get behind me. I see Satan in your eyes. I ain't afraid of Satan 'cause my God is stronger." She raised her hand and closed her eyes and prayed, "Satan. Leave my friend. Leave this house. This house does not belong to you." I began to tremble; so hard I spilled my soothing pills on the floor. Then, I became limp and passed out on the bed.

The next thing I recall was Linnie standing over me; very much the same as when I had the concussion from the wreck on Old Telegraph Road. This time, Linnie's breath was fresh and clean and the look in her eyes was warm and tender. I sat up to take a sip of the cool water she lovingly offered. Yes, it was only water. No syringe full of valium and no liquor in the glass. The coolness of the water was soothing to my throat. I thanked Linnie and then came to my senses.

I realized it was time for me to get to work. I sat up and was immediately fully conscious. I said, "Linnie, help me get ready for work by making me a lunch. I will get dressed. I only have a few minutes to make it to work before I am late, again." Linnie quickly moved to the kitchen and I heard her making my sandwich and pouring steaming hot coffee into my thermos.

I wasn't late to work. I was on time and I was there without my drugs in my bloodstream. I worked a full shift and was tired when I returned home. Linnie was waiting for me; she had her

Bible in her lap and was reading it. When she saw me she smiled and said, "How did it go at work? It looks like you are tired out and ready to sleep." I nodded in agreement; got a drink of water and fell into bed. I slept from early morning until late the next day. That was the best sleep I had since we found Ornella in the street. I didn't dream about running and hiding from the black funnel cloud that watched me, ready to reach down and torture me.

For many more weeks, Linnie didn't give up on me. She continued to read me passages from the Bible whenever we were together. She knew where and what I was still doing on the weekends with my clients. I politely listened. You see, God was calling me to ask for forgiveness so He could release me from the stronghold Satan had on me. Sadly, I didn't call out to Him until much later. Although, the most remarkable thing during those days was I didn't need my friends – the drugs that numbed my senses. I didn't understand that the Holy Spirit had taken away my desire for the drugs.

My craving for drugs was gone because I had been healed by the Holy Spirit. It happened the first time Linnie held me and comforted me. That was when I felt the Holy Spirit touch my heart. I was grateful I had been freed of my addition, even though I wasn't sure how it happened. I didn't ask for it or expect it. Linnie was very aware of what had happened, so she continued to read the Bible to me and to pray with me. Her goal was to help me understand the miracle that God showered on me; just as He had blessed her. She was patient because she understood that it would take a long time to fill-in-the gap of my knowledge of God and His love for me.

Slowly and lovingly she kept reading to me and praying for me. She knew it would take time to soften my heart because it had been cold and hard for many years. As I listened to her, I still wanted to be in control because I did not know how to release my fears to God. I wasn't ready to surrender; not yet. Although, my attitude toward Christians slowly began to improve. Seeing the dramatic transformation in Linnie revealed to me that people can change. I began to ponder, maybe, just maybe, I had a chance.

My change started gradually. Slowly, I began to consider to stop meeting my men clients. Such a dramatic lifestyle change would be a threat to Satan. He would put up a hard fight to keep me living in sin. He knew his hold over me was in jeopardy. In defense, he put together his army to strike and this time much harder. Satan alerted his demons. They had another, more sinister and deadly plan for me. Once more, his demon-filled funnel cloud was on the prowl. What I failed to see was that God was standing with me, ready to wrap me in His arms and protect me. Why did I not see Him? Why was I blind to God? Oh, how I needed to open my eyes and turn toward God.

And, the hunt began. Satan's deadly funnel cloud was released and his plot of destruction was soon to be revealed.

". . . Submit yourselves therefore to God. Resist the devil, and he will flee from you."
(James 4:7 KJV)

Chapter 5

The Hunt

The hunt was on. I was the hunted and Satan and his army of demons were the hunters. I was their victim who didn't understand the power and Glory of our creator God. I wasted many years running from God; not realizing He was waiting for me. All I needed to do was turn around and see Him and my running would be over. I was a victim of prison thinking; confused and distressed by Satan's lies. I was a hostage of Satan and was headed for an early death. As I drifted deeper and deeper into Satan's black abyss, he carefully waited. His lies, laced with his poison had kidnapped my soul. His deception gripped me tighter and tighter. To try to be free of his grasp, I ran and ran; believing my journey would end with the peace I desired. I didn't understand that I was running in the wrong direction. I was running away from the Truth and Light; Yeshua HaMashiach – Jesus, the Anointed One.

My running could have ended, if only I had opened my ears and eyes I would have known Yeshua was calling me. If only I had been running in a different direction. If only I had listened more sincerely to Linnie as she read to me from the Bible. If only I had taken the hand of Jesus as He stood beside me. If only I had believed the Truth of the Scriptures. Instead, in my blindness and deafness, I continued to follow the liar, Satan. I was walking the path to hell because Satan knew my weakness. He took advantage of my ignorance and he and his army were on the hunt for another soul to destroy. I was the hunted.

The scriptures Linnie read to me clearly explained Satan and his war with God. Yeshua, the *Truth* that has been alive before the Earth and the universe was created. He is Our Savior and Glorious Son of God. I had heard the truth; but I did not listen or accept it. I believed I didn't need God. I thought that I could be in control of my life. After all, I had done a fairly good job of fleeing my past. I ran because I thought I had been abandoned by God. I was so wrong, He was always with me.

If I had turned and acknowledged God's presence and asked for forgiveness, my past would have been immediately forgiven and erased. I would never again be tormented by the guilt and shame of it. I would be free to breathe, laugh, love, trust and live in peace. Yeshua, my protector; the father I needed. He was ready to adopt me as His child. I would finally have a father that loved and protected me. If only. Yes, if only. My lack of faith and reluctance to believe opened the door of hell. I was standing in front of it. The hunt was on to drag me into it.

This is how the hunt began. While working late one night at the local bar, I glanced around the room to see if anyone needed a refill or if there were new customers. I noticed a strange and sinister figure hiding at a corner table. He looked vaguely familiar. He was dressed in a long black overcoat that hid his clothes. His hat was old and worn and reminded me of a dirty cowboy hat. It was pulled down over his forehead. I couldn't see all of his face. He had a full beard and mustache. It was black and curly. His black hair, greasy and long, hung around his neck. As I eyed him, I felt a cold shudder run down my spine. Instinctively I turned away from him because I felt I was in danger. I decided to escape by walking to the end of the bar.

Once there, I asked the bartender if he knew the stranger. He casually glanced at him. He smiled at me and said, "Nope." Keeping from looking at the strange man, I stared at the bartender a few minutes and asked, "I don't want to wait on him. Do you mind if I take a break in the back room. Can you wait on him? I don't like the look of him." He smiled again, and replied,

"Anything for you. I don't want my best waitress getting ruffled by a nasty looking stranger. I can take care of him, if you know what I mean?" I nodded and hurriedly escaped to the backroom. Once out of sight of the stranger, I felt safe in the backroom. The small room was where the cooks and dishwashers worked. They were a close knit and fun group. They took care of each other and would take care of me if I needed the help.

When I walked in one of the older workers noticed me. His name was Hank. He was about medium height with strong muscular arms and a bulky rock-hard chest. He was from Texas; half American Indian and half Irish. He spoke with a thick Texas accent. He came to meet me. He took my tray of empty glasses and put them on a table. He held my arm; I hadn't realized I was shaking. He said, "Nina. You were shaking so hard when you came in I thought you was gonna' drop them glasses. What is going on little lady?"

I couldn't speak. My throat was suddenly dry. He responded to my silence, "Let me help you sit down. Your face is as white as snow. Are you feeling sickly?" I answered in a pitifully faint voice, "Yes. Yes, I am. I think I looked the devil right in the eye tonight." That got the

74

attention of everyone in the room and it got deadly silent.

Everyone stopped working and they grabbed chairs and joined us at the table. One young man asked, "Sure 'nuf? The devil himself is here tonight. If that ain't something. I want to get a look at him." Then he laughed, a silly naïve laugh. Another small, older man gave him a cautionary look. He was from the Florida swamps and was part Cajun and part African-American. His dark skin was covered with freckles and his hair was a medium brown. It was kept in a long braid down his back. He wore colorful jewelry; some fashioned from animal bones.

He spoke in a low and warning tone, "Don't take this lightly, youngster. The devil ain't nothing to take carelessly. He got lots of power and can do you deadly harm." The young man laughed and said, "Old man. You and your superstitious black-magic religion. I ain't afraid of no man-devil. You believe in spooks. They ain't no spook I can't take on." The Cajun shook his head in disbelief. He warned the young man, "Don't be braggin'. The evil spirits will hear you. They don't take kindly to your kind of talk."

75

While all this was happening, I sat there, rigid from fear. I heard their voices, but I didn't understand what was said. My mind was blank and my heart was beating so fast I felt dizzy. Hank moved his chair closer to me. He asked in a caring and fatherly tone, "Little lady. You don't look so good. This here fella out there, he got you real spooked. Do you know him? Has he done you harm?" I strained a look at Hank and answered, "What did you say?"

He repeated his statement, this time with a firm voice. My head began to clear and I understood him. I answered while all the others intently watched me and waited for my response. I said, in almost a whisper, "He reminds me of someone very evil. Someone from my past. Someone I thought I would never see again."

They began to whisper among themselves. They were saying things like, "Let's go out there and run him off." Another said, "Naw. Let's watch him and follow him. Then when he is outside, let's grab him and rough him up." The Cajun spoke up, "If he is the devil, himself, we need to think this out. He could turn on us an cast a bad spell on all of us. We could all be dead by morning."

This time, the young man didn't laugh. He stared at the Cajun and started to sweat. He asked, "Do ya'll take this voodoo devil stuff serious like cause ya'll are given me the willies." Then Hank answered, "I don't know about voodoo stuff, but I know a lot about the devil. He can show up looking like anybody or anything. He is always hunting for some innocent soul to rip apart and kill. He might be on the prowl tonight and none of us want to be his next victim."

After he warned them they began to mutter among themselves and went back to work. I felt as if the room was suddenly thick with fear. As I sat there not knowing what to do, the bartender came in. He sat beside me and asked, "Do you feel like coming back to work? The regulars are asking for you. I can't satisfy them; they want your pretty face delivering their dinner and drinks. " I raised my head and stared at his face. He leaned back as if he had seen a ghost. "What is going on here? Hank, have all of you been spookin' her? Tell me what's been said, right now."

Hank looked at the bartender and answered, "We just been warning her about evil-lookin' strangers. She ought to stay away from them and not wait on them. We need to protect our own, you know." The bartender shook his head in disbelief and disgust. He angrily answered, "I should have all of you fired. I bet you scared Miss Nina to death with your voodoo nonsense." When he said 'death', everyone turned their backs to him, put their heads down, went back to their tasks and stayed silent. I felt as if I was marked for something very evil.

The bartender saw their reaction and said, "Hank. You walk her home. Go out the back way. Get the pistol from the cabinet; it's loaded but on safety. Make sure she gets home safe and that her house is locked tight. I doubt if the stranger in the black coat will do her any harm. I talked to him. He was just passing through. He is from the deep south and said he was a swamp man." When he said 'swamp man' I began to shake. I remember screaming; but what I said, I don't remember. I recall Hank grabbing my arm, getting the gun and rushing out of the kitchen with me. As he walked me home, he held my arm with a tight grip.

All the way home I was crying and shaking. When we reached the house, Linnie wasn't there. She was working a night shift at the hospital. Since Ornella had died, she worked only when she was needed. I was alone and in need of my pills. Hank gave me two of them with a drink of water. He waited until I was asleep before leaving. He locked everything before leaving then he searched the neighborhood for any sign of the stranger.

With the help of my drugs, I slept all that night and most of the next day. Linnie came home around daylight. She had no knowledge of what had happened at my job. She noticed I was sleeping peacefully and didn't wake me until close to dinner time. When I awoke, I smelled food cooking and realized I was very hungry. I felt better and what happened the previous night seemed like a bad dream. I didn't mention any of it to her. I just didn't know how to tell her; the thought of sharing the pain and anguish of my younger years was too difficult. Talking about it flooded me with the horrible memories.

Later that evening, Hank came by before going to work at the bar. Linnie was surprised to see a strange man stop by the house. She asked me if I knew him and I said I worked with him at the bar. Realizing he wasn't a stranger, she graciously invited him in. She offered Hank a glass of tea or a cup of coffee. He chose the coffee and drank it as we three sat at the kitchen table.

After a few minutes of small talk, Hank asked, "Are you feeling better Miss Nina?" I nodded a yes, but I didn't speak. Linnie gave me a questioning look, then turned to Hank and said, "What did you say? Was Nina sick? I wish I had known. I thought she was just sleeping 'cause she was tired. Nina, why didn't you tell me you were sick? You know I am here to help you in any way I can." Hank replied, "She had a might hard scare last night. We all did. There was a nasty-looking stranger in the bar last night. He frightened Miss Nina right out of her mind. She cried and shook all the way home. She was saying, 'The snake. Get the snake.'"

Then he added, "She kept trying to break away from me. She scratched my arm something fierce. See the scratches?" I looked at the deep, red scratches on his forearm. I said, "Hank. I am so sorry. I don't remember any of it. I was out of my head, crazy." Hank laughed, "Yes, ma'am. You were really crazy actin', for sure. I drug you home, kickin' and screamin'. No doubt about it, the neighbors heard and saw it all. I got you in bed and gave you them pills you wanted. They worked right off and you was sleepin' in no time. Then I locked the house tight, took a good look around and went right back to work. When I got back, the stranger was gone. I hope he left town and don't come back." I answered, "I hope so, too."

He patted my hand and asked, "Will you be coming to work tonight. The boss wants to know. He ain't got no one else to call. The other waitress is sick and ailin'. He needs you something fierce." I said, "Yes. Will you wait for me while I get dressed?" He quickly answered, "You betcha. The boss said I was to walk you to and from work for a long time. He wants to make sure you feel safe." His answer helped me relax but, deep inside I knew the stranger didn't leave. He was watching and waiting for the right time to strike.

The hunt was on and the evil funnel cloud was prowling and planning its attack. I was the helpless prey; I had no way to protect myself. I was an easy target. I had to find a way to defend myself, or to strike first. I decided I should tell Linnie my story because she was also in danger. My wicked brother was in town and he would do whatever he could to hurt me. If Linnie stood between us she was in danger, too. It was time for me unpack my hidden past; it was time to reveal it to the only person I trusted, Linnie.

Those thoughts stayed with me as I went to work that night. That shift, I kept a close watch to see if he had returned. He hadn't. I was relieved; I was safe, for the moment. After work, Hank walked me home with the loaded pistol in his pocket. He was ready to pull it and shoot it, if needed. I made it home safely and this time Linnie was waiting for me. Linnie was sitting at the kitchen table; coffee and Bible in her hands.

As Hank walked me into the house, it looked as if she had been praying or reading her Bible. Linnie turned toward us; I saw that her eyes were swollen and red. She had been crying. I knew she was worried about me. The time was right to tell her about my brother and why he was in town. Hank asked, "If you two ladies don't mind. I would like to stay a few minutes; just to be sure no one followed us."

I answered, "Hank. I was going to ask you to stay. I have something I need to tell both of you. You both need to know what this is all about. Hank, please pull up a chair. I will get you some coffee?" I walked over to the sink and saw the reflection of my face in the window. I thought I was looking at me as a little girl; a scared little girl crying for my mama. I pulled the curtains shut, let out a moan, and poured the coffee for Hank.

After we were sitting at the table, I began to share my story. As I talked, I looked at my hands. They were shaking. I didn't notice I was crying until I saw tears drop onto them. At first just a few fell. Then, they poured like big-hot raindrops. I didn't wipe them off; I let the tears drench my hands. It was as if my tears were filled with the pain of my childhood. I kept talking until everything was said. Suddenly, I stopped with nothing more to say. I began to feel weak and was incredibly tired. Linnie saw the change in me. She said, "Nina, I think you need me and God right now".

Linnie walked behind me and wrapped her arms around my shoulders. She began to rock me back and forth and whispered a soothing prayer. Hank sat silently and respectfully as we two women tried to reverse our agony. At that moment, I believed she felt my pain and her nearness made me feel protected and loved. The two of us cried until there were no more tears. Then, we were silent. After a few seconds of silence, Linnie returned to her chair. She handed me an old-ragged kitchen towel and I wiped the tears from my face and hands.

Hank cleared his throat and said he had something to tell us. He said he would keep us safe. He said, "I won't leave either of you women. I don't have a family or anything. I lost everything when I went to prison. I came here to get away from my bad past. The only family I have is those at the bar. If you don't object to having an old-worn out Texan around, I would like to stay here and watch over the place if you need me." Linnie answered, "It has been many years since a man has shared a house with me. It would be good to have you here. I guess no one objects, we aren't women with untainted backgrounds."

Hank sat up straight and leaned forward, "I ain't here to take advantage of you women. I am here to guard your place from her brother. I can sleep outside in the shed. All I need is a cot and blanket. I got good hearin'and I got a good watch dog. I will bring him with me and if anyone is sneakin' around, well, he won't like what my dog will do." When I heard that, I relaxed and began to laugh. We all laughed that night; it felt good. Hank continued to guard me and Linnie as we waited for the devil and his demons to attack.

Hank moved into our dirty, leaky shed. He brought his dog; it was part German Shephard and Rot Wyler. His name was Gator. It matched him well. He was Hank's dog, for sure. He obeyed Hank and loved him. It took a few days before Linnie and I were comfortable around

him. Once he took to us, he was our dog, too.
Hank kept the loaded pistol close by and
continued to walk me to and from work.

Since we both worked nights, he slept during
most of the day. Knowing Hank was a light
sleeper and Gator was a great watchdog, Linnie
and I began to relax. We felt as if we were fully
protected from my brother. When Hank was up
and about, he worked on the shed, made repairs
and turned it into a decent place to sleep. He
added a small wood-burning stove so he could
make his coffee and hot water for shaving. He
bought a tin tub to bath in. He said he liked his
privacy and wasn't one to bathe in a woman's
house. He said he enjoyed being outside most of
the time; staying inside reminded him of prison.

We never asked Hank why he was in prison.
It must have been something serious because his
family left him. They never made any attempt to
find him. I guess we three were the same. We
were displaced people with no close family ties.
Linnie lost her daughter, I lost my mama and
Hank lost even more. He told us he had a son
who would be about thirty years old. He said he
was broken hearted that he didn't get to see him
grow up to be a man.

85

He never told us about his wife or any of his other family. We thought it best no to intrude into his personal affairs; we never asked him about them. We knew it was too painful for Hank to talk about the past. We had a lot in common because our past made us sad and lonely. The three of us became a family of sorts. Not blood related; but connected by our former lives of pain and loss. We also could protect and help each other. Unknown to us, we had a common enemy; the hunter who was gathering his army. There were two other enemies who were traveling across the county and soon to arrive; my other two brothers.

After the night when I saw one brother at the bar, he never returned. He moved into a shack in the country not far from Old Telegraph Road. It was the abandoned adobe farm house also known as the stagecoach rest stop. He found it to be livable with the water well still standing and working. The shack was secluded and a good place to hide-out because it was surrounded by an abandoned almond orchard. It was close to the old oak tree whose branches still hung over Old Telegraph Road.

After the deadly wreck of the 1960s that injured me, the area was almost always deserted. The memory of that night kept people away.

Town gossip was the place was haunted with ghosts of outlaws that were hung from the old oak tree. Since the awful wreck, only a few broken down farm trucks traveled the road. My brother had chosen a good place to hide and wait for the arrival of my other brothers. It wasn't too long until they arrived.

Once reunited, they planned to kidnap, torture and kill me; the sister whom they hated for many years. They discovered where I had escaped to when a stranger came to their part of the swamp. He was looking for an exciting vacation. He talked a lot and gave them the information they had been seeking since I escaped. It was the missing clue they needed to locate their runaway sister. As he spoke, they intently listened and the hate they had stored for me would soon be released.

He was a businessman from a farming area in California's central valley. He owned orchards, grape vineyards and had his own packing and shipping sheds. He was very wealthy and could buy anything he wanted. One thing he liked, was pretty young prostitutes. Since he lived in a small town, good prostitutes were hard to find. Although, he knew two women who were just what he liked. One was a little wild and enjoyed drinking and shooting up heroin and other drugs.

He lost her when she died from a supposed overdose.

The second woman was younger and had a southern drawl; similar to the Deep South. She was tall, muscular and strong for a woman with deep blue eyes and hair as black as coal. She knew a lot about snagging alligators and living in the swamps. She had a serious hatred of snakes and she knew how to kill and cook them. He said that as a child, a snake had tried to strangle her. Hearing about the snake interested the brothers, and they asked him to share more about the pretty prostitute.

He said that she lived outside of town and worked in a local bar as a cocktail waitress. Her name was Nina. It was short for Carolina. Instantly, her brothers knew their search for Nina had ended. Now, they could easily find her so she could get what she deserved. They figured the trip across country would take some good planning. So, they decided to send one brother by bus so he could get a good look around. He was also to find a place where they could stay and be free from the eyes of the law. Especially, since the other two brothers would bring dynamite, rifles and guns. Now, they needed money to make it happen.

While planning, the three hunted and rounded up a good haul of pelts and alligator hides. They got enough money from the sale of their kills and were able to send one brother by bus. Once the first brother was settled, he was to mail a letter with a map to his hideout. Then, the other two brothers would buy a used truck, get a couple of road maps and head out. With their stash of money they bought a rundown truck and drove over two-thousand miles in it. During their long trip, they concocted their plan.

They were excited about putting it into action. It was to be one of their best hunting trips; evil enough to satisfy their pagan appetite for murder and bloodshed. Their victim, Nina, would be stalked for a few days; plenty of time to make her worry. That would give them time to identify her friends so they could add them to their hunt. Slowly, they would surround her home to taunt her with threats of torture.

Yes, even her friends would be surrounded and tortured. It would be a great hunt that promised many victims with many hours of satiating brutality that they craved. Their pagan desires would be filled as they slowly killed them. The dead would be burned and then buried in the countryside; not far from the old adobe shack. It was a perfect plan. They were anxious to get started.

While their sinister plans were being made, God had His own plan. He was surrounding Nina with those he chose to protect her. Linnie was chosen to pray for her and lead her to God. Hank was there to provide his strong arms and body to fend off those who would do her harm. Gator was there to warn when prowlers were roaming about. He was preparing His army of angels to defend his child. Nina was to be protected from Satan's plan to take her life and her soul. God's plan is always perfect.

In the midst of all this, Nina desperately needed to turn around and stop running toward Satan. God was close; very close. All she had to do was reach out to touch the hand of God. Linnie knew this and she desperately wanted to help Nina understand she wasn't alone and that God was always with her. How was she going to do it? The only thing Linnie knew to do was to go to God in prayer; fervent prayer each and every day. She begged, pleaded, and cried for Nina. As she prayed, her heart and soul were poured into her prayers. During those times she could hear her inner voice pleading, "Dear God. Don't take my Nina. I lost my Ornella. I can't lose Nina too."

Linnie had been praying that Nina would give up her prostituting and she couldn't understand why she wouldn't let it go. One night, Nina walked into the house with a strange look on her face. It was a look of sheer terror. Linnie ran to her and cried out, "Have you been injured? Did someone hurt you? Oh Nina, tell me what is wrong!" Nina slowly walked away from her and sat in a chair that faced the front window. Linnie immediately felt a pang of dread. Her Nina was in shock and she needed to know why. Linnie watched in agony as Nina walked away from her and toward the window that faced the street.

Nina stood and stared out the window as if looking for someone. Then she pulled up a chair and slowly sat in it. Her movements were stiff and reminded Linnie of a robot. When Nina sat in the chair, her eyes were probing and searching. She seemed to be checking the neighborhood for something. Linnie pulled her from the window and turned Nina so they could face each other. Nina seemed to be in a trance. She grabbed Nina by the shoulders and tried to shake her free of her stupor. Nothing helped. She yelled at her with no response. Linnie began to panic and screamed for Hank.

The Effigy

*"When I kept silence, my bones waxed old through
my roaring all the day long."*
(Psalm 32:3 KJV)

Hank heard Linnie. He and Gator rushed to
the house. Gator was barking and growling,
eager to pounce upon who and what was causing
his friends such grief. Linnie cried to Hank, "It's
Nina. I can't get her to see me. I think she is in
shock. Don't let Gator in – he might bite her."
Hank answered, "Don't fret, I got him. I think he
can smell or sense something close; something
really bad. There may be someone lurking
around. We need him to find who or what it is."
Linnie yelled back, "Hold him tight!"

With a tight rein on Gator, Hank slowly
opened the door as he talked calmly to Gator. He
said, "It's alright Gator. The ladies aren't hurt.
Keep still and don't break from me." Gator
immediately stopped barking and changed to a
menacing growl. His ears were flat and his tail
was down. He crept into the house slowly and
looked from side to side; he was searching for the
unseen enemy. His keen dog senses knew the
enemy was close at hand.

Linnie was relieved and said, "Good Gator.
Good Gator. Protect my Nina." As if he

92

understood, he crawled over to Nina and lay down by her feet. Nina looked down at Gator then fell back into the chair. Her limp hand landed on his back. Gator moved closer to her to lick her hand as if to reassure her he would keep her safe. Hank asked, "Linnie. What went on here?" She answered in a more controlled but still panicky voice, "Something happened with a client. She was with one of them tonight. I begged her not to go; I begged her to quit. It ain't safe with her brother prowling about; but she went anyway." Hank didn't answer. He walked backwards and said, "I am going to look over the place real good for anything different. It might be that her brother was watching the place and maybe left something to scare her. I don't know what I might dig up, but I will know it when I see it. You stay close to Nina. You will be safe with Gator; no one in their right mind will come up on Gator."

Hank scoured the house, the yard, the street and adjacent houses. He returned holding a small object in his hand. He showed it to Gator. Gator smelled it and growled menacingly. Hank took the object and showed it to Linnie; it was a voodoo effigy made to look like Nina. There was a knife in its back. Linnie put her hand over her mouth and gasped. The knife was embedded in the same place Ornella had been stabbed.

93

Linnie stepped backwards and lost her footing. Hank leaped forward and caught her before she fell. She gasped, "That was how my Ornella died. She didn't die from an overdose, she was stabbed in the back." Hank answered, stunned by what she said. He slowly replied, "What? Are you sure? That ain't what the cops said."

Linnie looked down at her trembling hands, then she gasped for air and said, "If I were still drinking hard liquor, I would need one right now. But I ain't doing it no more. Can you pour me a cup of hot coffee from the stove. I got to have a strong cup or I will faint this very minute." Hank was happy to oblige. He helped her to the kitchen table, pushed her chair in then got her the coffee. It was good and strong.

Linnie put cream and sugar in it and drank it down in one swallow. When finished, she leaned forward and prayed, "Lord. Help us. Satan has surrounded us. The enemy is near." Then she quoted the Bible, "He delivered me from my strong enemy, and from them which hated me: for they were too strong for me." She told Hank it was Psalm 18:17 when David was surrounded by Saul, his enemy. She added that God delivered David from his enemy. She told Hank that God could surely do the same for them.

Linnie added, "As my preacher says, 'Our God is a prayer-hearing God and I am a praying woman. Well, we are all in need of God, right now.'" Hank nodded in agreement and said, "Yes ma'am. All of us are in need of God cause what is hunting Nina is not just man, it is the devil's black magic. It's the kind that kills you even before you get stabbed in the back."

Linnie shivered when he spoke. Her body was filled with a foreboding of a future tragedy. She grabbed her coffee cup to ask for more, but her hand shook so hard she dropped it. It broke on the floor. Linnie noticed Nina didn't respond to the sudden sound of the crashing glass. Nina remained still and in a trance. "I guess maybe it is good that Nina don't know what is going on," Hank said in a concerned voice. Then, Linnie started to pick up the glass but Hank put his hand on her arm to stop her.

He said, "Let me help. The way you is shaking, you will just break another one and probably get a bad cut. I will get it and pour you another cup. Looks like this is gonna' be a long night for both of us. Nina is in different world and we don't know when she will return." Linnie said, "Yes. You are right. I guess we need to leave her alone. She will come back in God's

95

good time and I pray it will be soon. I can't take losing her." Hank answered, " I know. I know."

He swept the floor clean of broken glass and got Linnie another cup of strong-black coffee. He poured himself a cup and noticed he had drained the pot of what was left. He started another pot brewing on the old gas stove; the one Linnie and Ornella bought from the second hand store. It didn't look like much, but it worked and was good enough to cook their food and make their coffee. Hank put it to good use that night and for many more nights. The strong-black coffee was needed because Nina was to remain in her psychotic stupor for several days .

The next day, Nina had not left the chair. Linnie decided to call the local doctor. He made a house call and examined Nina. He shone a light into her eyes, listened to her lungs and heart, and snapped his fingers next to her ears. Nina did not respond. The doctor shook his head then said, "Something incredibly bad happened for her to be this way. We can't do anything for her but wait." Linnie began to softly cry. The doctor walked over to Linnie and said, "Don't try to wake her up; just keep her comfortable and try to get her to eat and drink something. Watch her closely so she doesn't choke when you feed her.

Call me if she doesn't come around in a few days. I may need to put her the hospital."

Linnie nodded her head to let him know she understood, then she turned her attention to Nina. Not wanting to alarm Linnie, Hank whispered something to the doctor before he left. The doctor got a surprised look on his face because Hank whispered to him about the effigy and the knife. With a seriously concerned expression, the doctor looked over his shoulder at Nina. He softly said something to Hank, then slowly walked to his car. As he drove back to his office his thoughts were about Ornella and the deep hole in her back. He wondered if the same person that killed Ornella was going to attack Nina. He thought he should tell the town sheriff about the effigy and his house call to check on Nina.

After the doctor left, Nina didn't change. She continued to stare out the window with eyes blank and fixed at the window. She remained in that state for a few days. During her stupor, she ate and drank only when Linnie forced food and water in her mouth. She didn't leave the chair to sleep in her bed; she slept irregularly and for very short time periods. All the while, Gator never left her side for more than a few moments.

He only left to get a drink, eat a few bites and go outside to relieve himself. He was her guardian from the unseen and unknown enemy that was lurking about attending to its evil plan. Her brothers were doing the same – they had reunited the week Hank found the voodoo effigy. Although, they were not the perpetrators who made it. There was another enemy; one they didn't know. One that was so close, they didn't see him. The Cajun was another of Satan's henchmen whose desire was to kill God's children.

Satan had a second plan to steal Nina's life and soul. He was preparing the Cajun to carry out his wickedness.

"Ye are of your father the devil, and the lusts of your father ye will do. He was a murderer from the beginning, and abode not in the truth, because there is no truth in him. When he speaketh a lie, he speaketh of his own: for he is a liar, and the father of it."
(John 8:44 KJV)

Chapter 6

The Steel Rod

The Cajun was an unusual man who lived a secluded life. He wasn't native to California; he was from the deep south. He traveled to the small farming town the same as many other town residents. He had been in serious trouble with the law while living in south Louisiana, in the French Quarters. He was French and Spanish. He spoke with a strange accent and it always seemed as if he spit out his words. When he talked, his mouth was almost closed except for one side. People said he talked like Popeye, the cartoon character. His voice was almost a growl and came from deep inside his throat. It was easy to recognize that he was different; some said he was just plain odd.

His outward appearance was as unique as his speech. He walked with a stiff and rapid gate. His body was thin and his legs were incredibly short. He didn't have much facial hair and often didn't shave. His thin-scraggly beard gave him a rough and shabby appearance. Most of the time, his clothes were wrinkled, stained and shabby. Grooming and cleanliness were not part of his daily routine. If he had been fishing at the local irrigation canal; he smelled of rotten fish bate and

101

body sweat. He also had an ugly smile that showed a mouth with few teeth; most broken from fights. He chewed tobacco and what teeth were left were stained brown. Overall, he was not pleasing to the eye or nose. Most people he was near kept their distance and were glad he lived outside of town.

His house was not far from Nina's brothers' shack. It was the old ranch-hand's adobe shed. The Cajun was prone to picking up trash and hording it. The outside of his shack had so much junk piled up, only the top of the shack was visible except for a rickety-wooden door that was the only entrance or exit. It wasn't unusual to see black smoke coming from his place. It was rumored that not only did he burn trash but sometimes animals that he killed as sacrifices.

How he ended up working at the bar was a mystery to all who worked there. Sometimes, he arrived stinking and in filthy rags. Thankfully, the owner of the bar made him bathe and change clothes. The owner of the bar was known to throw him a bar of soap and a garden hose. The Cajun didn't care, he would laugh and scrub in the cold water until the owner thought he was clean. The owner always had something on hand for the Cajun to wear after his cold bath. The employees at the bar were glad he bathed before starting work. They were grateful the owner made him do it, it made their job a lot more pleasant.

The employees said he felt sorry for the Cajun, that was why he gave him occasional work. He didn't do much; his duties were to sweep the parking lot, the alley, and the bar after it closed. For his work he got cheap whiskey, food, cigarettes or bags of tobacco. He also was known to steal and beg from local residents. He often talked about voodoo and the devil. Those he worked with at the bar often ignored or laughed at his warnings about evil spirits and spells. Also, no one suspected that he was dangerous and capable of murder.

Ornella avoided him and warned Nina to keep her distance. She said the Cajun didn't like women and he had a deep hate for prostitutes. She said his deceased mother had been a prostitute and he was the product of one of her Johns. Ornella didn't know his full story; if she had, she would have shared it with the owner and Nina. His story was one of gruesome cruelty and filled with vindictive hatred for all women; especially prostitutes.

He had been orphaned as a baby by his mother. The couple that raised him told him his father was a French seaman. They told him his mother often lived with him when his ship was in port. One particular time, he was in port for a couple of months. It was during those months she discovered she was pregnant. She told the French seaman she was carrying his child. In a drunken rage, he beat her and threw her into the street to die. His adoptive parents, who owned a small store, found her the next morning and took her in. They cared for his mother until she gave birth. After she was well, she left. They kept the baby because they had no children of their own. As the child grew, he always knew who his mother was. She never tried to see him so he watched her from a distance.

When he was about fifteen or sixteen, he ran away from home. He spent his time secretly following her. He stalked her and watched her as she met men. He sneakily followed them as she took them to her shabby hotel room. Once inside with the man, the Cajun would sit outside her room with his ear to the door. As he listened, his hate for his mother turned into murderous rage. To appease his growing anger, he sought the help of a voodoo priest. He told the priest he wanted her to suffer. The priest sold him a voodoo effigy of his mother. He kept it and stuck pins in it when she was with a John. In his mentally deranged and sick mind, he wanted her to be blind and helpless, so he stuck several pins in her eyes and legs. Eventually his mother lost her sight from a serious stroke that not only blinded her, but left her unable to walk. He was pleased.

While she was in a hospital, a filthy excuse for a hospital, he sat by her bedside. She would cry out for her son and he would answer, "Your son is here. He won't leave you like you left him." When she attempted to produce a smile from her disfigured face, he thought she looked like a witch. Overtime, he began to believe she was a witch. One night he came to the hospital with matches and the voodoo effigy of his mother. He lay the effigy on her bed and set it on fire.

Within a few moments, her entire bed was engulfed in flames. He stood silently by as she screamed for help. The nurses and staff tried valiantly to douse the flames and save her. It was no use; she died from inhaling the searing flames that covered her crippled body. The police came and took him to jail. He was pronounced incompetent, served a few years in jail then released. Eventually, he made his way to the same small town in which Nina lived.

Once settled outside of town on Old Telegraph Road; not far from the Old Oak Tree.

He found work, begged or stole when he needed tobacco, whiskey or food. While working at the bar, he pretended to be friendly and seemed harmless. In reality, he was a monster. He murdered Ornella because of what she was; a prostitute. She sold her body so she could feed her consuming appetite for heroin. Each time she shot the soothing poison into her body, it screamed for more. Never satiated, it controlled her life. It was a love affair that cost her to pay the supreme price; her life. She would die at the hands of the deranged Cajun.

His lust for murder was driven by his hatred for his mother. When he killed Ornella, he imagined he was killing his mother. As she lay on the pavement after his attack, her blood flowed until her heart stopped. He was close by, watching. Ornella was not shot in the back as Nina thought. Even the cops and the doctor knew the hole in her back was not caused by a gun. There was no bullet and the hole was too big for a gunshot.

Due to its size, they were perplexed as to what caused it and also who did it. They never suspected the murderer was the short, smelly Cajun who talked and walked like a cartoon character. The gaping hole was made when he shoved a smooth-steel rod into her back. It went in easily because he had ground one end into a sharp point. He knew it would work because many small farm animals had died the same way. The Cajun had tested it on them; the ones that roamed freely in the foothills close to his hut. The ones that made the black smoke that curled upward from his shack. Convinced he would be successful, he waited for Ornella; he was ready to rid the town of a no-good prostitute.

The night she died, he followed her to a hotel and sat outside her room. He had done this many times before without being caught. That night was no different. He sat quietly by the door and listened. His hate grew into a fury. He couldn't wait to act out his plan. During the dark-early morning he heard her get ready to leave. He slithered away and hurried to the regular bus she took. He sat hidden in the back. The Cajun looked out the bus window and watched her step onto the bus.

He slipped lower in the seat as he muffled a vicious laugh. She sat in the front, the same as she always did. The bus started and during the ride he heard her talking to the bus driver. That night, as usual, the bus driver told her he would drop her off, close to her street. He told her he didn't want her to walk a long way; she would be much safer walking a only short distance. She thanked the bus driver and they talked and laughed as he drove.

It made the Cajun sick to his stomach to hear her laughing and joking. He thought she was stupid to laugh because soon she would be dead. Yes, stupid. She thought she would make it home without a problem. After all, how many times before had he watched and followed her? Many times, never to be detected. If she had been a smart woman, she would have seen him, at least once. Yes, she was stupid and careless.

He took a deep and satisfying breath; he was going to get rid her. His thoughts were abruptly interrupted as the bus jerked to a stop. He peered around the seat in front of him. He saw her stand up and walk out. He jumped up and ran to the door; the bus driver almost shut it on him. He jerked, turned to him and sneered. He said, "Open it dummy. Don't ya' know I got to git off!" The bus driver scowled at him; he was glad the smelly-little man was leaving. He thought him a nuisance, never a murder.

When the Cajun stepped off, the air was cold and the town was quiet. It was early morning and still dark. The streets were vacant. He knew there would be no witnesses. He ran to a side alley to run ahead of her. He was perfectly positioned as he waited for her to turn on her street. As she rapidly walked toward home, Ornella was unaware he was behind her. Quickly and quietly he leaped out of the darkness. He grabbed her around the neck and in one smooth motion, shoved the cold steel rod into her back. She didn't scream, just shuddered and then went limp. He laughed and dropped her to the pavement. He looked around. No lights were on in the houses. He turned and silently slinked into the darkness like a venomous snake.

A couple of hours later a car full of drunken teens found her stiff and cold body. As they drove down her street, it was almost day light. They noticed something unusual lying in the street. They slammed the brakes to a stop, then the staggering teens scrambled out. They huddled around the lump and saw that it was a woman. Looking closer, they recognized her. In their drunken state, they threw her body into the back seat. They knew where she lived on the street and drove to her house. Once there, they screeched to a stop. Full of liquor, they dropped her in the street. To them she was just another piece of trash. They didn't have the decency to move her off the street. As they drove off, not realizing the gravity of what they had done, all that was heard was the sound of their tires squealing; this woke Linnie and Nina.

Her death was ruled a drug overdose. A few weeks after her death, one of the teens spilled his guts to some friends about finding her. The teen was worried he could get caught, so he decided to go to the police and tell them what happened. After he was questioned, the remaining teens were rounded up and interrogated. Each teen told the same story. The police believed them. It was decided to keep their names quiet to protect the kids from the murderer. They also chose not to release how she was killed. How she died was the one piece of evidence that could convict the real butcher. The best way to catch whoever it was to wait. If the weapon showed up, they could recover fingerprints and possibly locate the criminal.

They didn't know the murderer was planning to kill a third victim. The Cajun, emboldened by his first two successes, was ravenous with power and planned to strike again. His twisted and perverted mind settled on Nina. Yes, he thought. She was perfect and because he was never questioned, he knew he would be successful. After all, the cops would think her brothers did it and everyone at the bar, where he worked, were buzzing about the strangers.

When the first brother moved into the shack, not far from Old Telegraph Road, the Cajun spied on him. The Cajun was more convinced after he searched their shack and discovered their arsenal of weapons and explosives. He sat outside the thick walls of the adobe shack and waited for him to leave. Once safely alone, he rummaged through it. He found their letters and read the contents. He learned about their plans to kidnap and torture Nina. Yes, he thought, they would be the perfect suspects. There was one thing he didn't know, Gator got his scent from the effigy of Nina. Hank found it and gave it to Gator. Gator was waiting.

The Cajun's filthy hands left his rotten body odor deeply embedded in it. Gator saved the scent in his brain and was ready to attack whoever or whatever matched the scent. You see, God goes before us. Sometimes we feel we are lost and wandering in a dark and lonely place; but God is always with us. That was where Nina was as she sat at the window. In her stupor, she was lost and running. God was there all the time; he was protecting Nina, even if she didn't know it.

A Deadly Mistake

Ready to strike his next victim; the Cajun prepared with malicious delight. He retrieved the steel rod, washed Ornella's blood from it and carried it under his arm. He stood it by the door of his hovel so he could see it and talk to it. He told the steel rod how delighted he was with it. It was strong, straight and deadly. The perfect weapon. It made no noise and was incredibly successful. He was well pleased with it. Oh yes, he was anxious for the two of them to strike one more time; maybe more. Partners they were to cleanse the world of stupid women. Full of evil bravado, the Cajun set out one night; it was a night darkened with thick-cold fog. He knew everyone would be inside their homes. It was too cold and wet to be outside. What he didn't know was that Gator was on alert.

That cold, foggy night, Gator never left Nina. During the late-night hours, Gator detected someone close by; someone evil. He lifted his head and sniffed the air. It smelled like the effigy. Gator waited for the scent to move closer. Unknowing Gator was scenting him, the Cajun jumped a fence and slinked down the street. Careful not to make a lot of noise, he only wore socks. They became wet and heavy from the fog. He tore them off and threw them into the street.

Gator, stood up. The scent was stronger and much closer. Now, the Cajun was barefoot and felt the cold-wet pavement as he slowly crept toward Nina's house. He liked the feel of it; it energized him. His mouth was set in his crooked smile; tobacco spit dribbled onto his chin. Wanting to laugh but knowing he should keep silent, he softly chuckled deep inside his throat. The denseness of the fog swallowed the noises he made. Although, Gator's keen hearing heard the stranger's chuckle. He began to growl.

Propelled by his insanity, the Cajun continued. He was confident he would be successful. As he crept closer to Nina's house, his twisted mind kept replaying the images of his mother burning. Reliving her death, gave him wicked pleasure. That night, Satan was on the prowl as he filled the Cajun with power and courage. That night, the devil stormed the Cajun's soul with his hatred for God's creation. Satan was well pleased; another of God's beautiful creatures would die. Satan was delirious with power and anticipation and he shared it with the Cajun.

The Cajun stopped less than a couple of feet from the front yard of Nina's house. Gator was fully alert and waiting. Gator smelled him; even the dense fog couldn't hide the stench of the Cajun. He began to growl much louder. Nina was in a deep her stupor; unknowing of her surroundings and not able to react to Gator's warning growl. Hank was sleeping on the sofa.

Since Nina became paralyzed with fear, he had taken up residence on the sofa. He knew what the voodoo effigy of Nina meant; his pistol was always loaded and ready to shoot any intruder. He thought it would be her brother; the stranger he saw in the bar. He was the man that scared Nina; the one in black trench coat with the dirty-greasy hair. He was prepared for whatever he needed to do to protect Nina and Linnie.

Gator's growl became louder and more menacing. It startled Hank from his sleep. He sat up, immediately alert. He rushed to Gator and whispered, "What is it Gator? Is someone outside? What do you sense, what do you hear?" Gator stood tall with his tail straight out and his ears lying flat on his immense head. Then, he became deadly silent. He was intently listening and scenting. The acrid nastiness of the effigy was getting closer. He turned his head to the side and glared at the door.

Then he crawled over on his belly as if stalking prey. He grabbed the effigy and bit into it. With it in his immense mouth, he shook it then turned to give it to Hank. Hank took it and said, "Is it the person who made this?" As if he understood, Gator placed himself directly in front of the door. During those few moments, Linnie had been half asleep. Hearing Hanks voice and the growls of Gator, she woke to a start. Linnie jumped out of bed, grabbed her robe and ran into the kitchen.

She saw Gator at the door. Instinctively, she turned toward Nina. Nina's head was thrown back as she sat unaware of where she was or what was happening. Hank was standing off to the side of the door, waiting for someone or something to try and open it. Hank whispered, "Linnie. Douse the lights. Something or someone is outside. Keep the house dark so they can't see us. They must be watching Nina from the street." Linnie immediately turned off the kitchen light. Hank said, "Don't talk and don't move. Gator is tracking it. We don't want to confuse him by moving about." Linnie froze. The silence was deathly and lay heavy in the air. Fear grasped her as she stood looking at Nina.

Then, someone or something tried to open the door. Gator growled – a low, rumbling growl. Whoever or whatever was at the door moved away. Then, someone was looking in the window at Nina. The thin curtains were pulled. The Cajun squinted, it was difficult to clearly see her in the dark. Hank and Linnie saw a face move closer to the window. Gator didn't move or make a sound. He watched in silence for his

115

chance to charge. Hank recognized who was standing at the window; it was the Cajun.

His mind began to race. He thought, why was the Cajun staring at Nina and what was he trying to do? Wasn't the Cajun harmless? Was it just curiosity or sheer stupidity that he was roaming the neighborhood in the early morning darkness? It didn't make sense. Hank looked at the effigy of Nina. Yes. That was it. The Cajun believed in voodoo and he made it. He realized it meant certain and imminent danger for Nina.

Hank released the safety on the pistol. He waited for the Cajun to make the next move. Again, the door handle began to move and a thin piece of metal was slipped between the door jam and the lock. The Cajun turned the now unlocked door and carefully opened it. Gator was ready to strike. As the Cajun moved quietly through the doorway, he crept into the room. Gator didn't move or make a sound, not yet. In total darkness, the Cajun moved toward Nina. Like a flash of lightening, Gator jumped and grabbed the Cajun by the throat. He tore at him in a violent fury. The Cajun screamed and wrestled with the massive dog. Somehow, he broke free and was holding something shiny in his hand.

Linnie flipped on the kitchen light. The Cajun was trying to stab Gator with a long, thin shiny object. Hank aimed the pistol at the Cajun. He couldn't get a clear shot with Gator in the way. He yelled at Gator to back off. In the split second Gator backed away from him, the Cajun saw his opportunity to stab the attacking dog. Hank had a clear shot and he took it. The Cajun slumped to the floor. Gator didn't flinch at the shot, he kept his eyes locked on the Cajun. After a few seconds, Gator crawled over to the intruder who was bleeding from a chest wound. He sniffed him, then put his gigantic paw on his face. He looked over at Hank, and barked. It was a bark that signaled the enemy was down.

Linnie ran to Nina and Hank grabbed the sharp-steel rod. He looked at it then threw it by the door. He was relieved to see that there was no blood on it; Gator was not injured. He knelt beside Gator and hugged him. Linnie thought she heard Hank crying as he softly talked to Gator. Once beside Nina, Linnie noticed her eyes were open and focused. The sound of the pistol jerked Nina out of unconsciousness. Nina shook her head and grabbed it with her hands and began to scream.

Her loud piercing scream penetrated the foggy night with sheer terror. Linnie tried to

117

calm her as she held her in her arms. Nina was finally breaking free of her stupor. Linnie soothingly talked to her to quiet her; but it didn't help. Then, Nina began to shake and cry. Linnie continued her attempt to calm Nina, but she screamed and wailed even louder. While Linnie held Nina, Hank let go of Gator and kneeled beside the body of the Cajun.

Hank took his pulse. There was none. The Cajun was dead; shot straight through the heart. Gator didn't back away, he continued to watch the Cajun for any sign of movement. He was positioned to attack the prone Cajun if he moved. It seemed that within seconds, neighbors were running to the house. The gun shot and Nina's screams alerted the neighborhood that something terrible happened.

Within minutes, a lone police siren was heard in the distance; someone must have called the police. Then, things seemed to happen rapidly. The police arrived and pushed their way through the onlookers. They cautioned the nosy neighbors to stay clear of the house, if not, they could be arrested. Once inside, they asked a lot of questions. They took photos, measured things, and stood clear of Gator.

Gator wasn't interested in the police. He kept his vigil over the Cajun and the police didn't attempt to move him. They respected the big dog; wisely so. They stayed until the morning sun began to peak through the thick fog. Daylight revealed the house and yard were free of the nosy neighbors. Unable to see what was happening inside the house, they went back to their warm, dry homes. The yard and street were empty when the preliminary crime scene investigation was complete. No one was arrested although Hank's pistol was seized for evidence along with the steel rod. The Cajun was carried off by an ambulance and transported to the morgue to be examined and certified as dead. His body had a bullet in the heart. He had deep wounds on his neck and arms. They were evidence that Gator fiercely protected Nina from her attacker.

One of the local police officers stayed a few extra minutes. He made an interesting comment about the steel rod. He said, "I think this is the murder weapon that killed the other woman; your daughter, Ornella. We have been looking for it. When we took Ornella to the morgue we found a voodoo effigy in her purse. It was just like the one Hank gave us. I would bet it was the Cajun who killed her. Although, I guess we might never know since he is stone dead. But, if you ask me, I think we just solved one mystery that has been stuck in my head way too long."

He continued, "Ornella was a nice lady and didn't deserve to die the way she did. I think her killer got what he deserved tonight. I hand over my thanks to Gator and Hank." When he finished he shook hands with Hank and then asked if he could pet Gator. Hank said, "I think it is okay. Gator knows the difference between the enemy and friends." The policeman carefully approached Gator and rubbed his head. Gator stood proud and tall as the policeman showed his thanks. He left with these words, "That Cajun made a deadly mistake coming to this house. Gator did a right good job catching the killer." He turned, walked out the door, got in his police car and drove away.

Gator stood and watched the police car until it disappeared from sight. Then he turned and walked to Hank. He stood in front of Hank as if we wanted to say something, but couldn't. His ears were pointed upward and his tail was straight out. Hank kneeled down and said, "Gator, do you want to tell me something?" Gator seemed to understand. He bent his two front legs as if to kneel, put his giant head on his paws and seemed to be in a position of prayer.

Hank said, "I think Gator is telling us we ought to say a prayer of thanks to the Good Lord."

————————————

Defeated and wounded, Satan retreats for a short time, only to strike again.

"For thou, Lord, art good, and ready to forgive;
And plenteous in mercy unto all them that call
upon thee."
(Psalm 86:5 KJV)

Chapter 7

Time to Pray

The blast from Hanks' gun had broken the spell that held Nina prisoner. Once on her feet, she reached for Linnie's arm and started to walk; feebly at first. With Linnie's help, Nina walked to the kitchen table where Linnie gave her a cup of strong, hot coffee. As Nina drank it, she felt the dark-warm liquid caress her dry throat. Nina let out a soft 'umm' to express her pleasure with the soothing coffee. Immediately, Linnie knew her Nina was returning.

She gently touched Nina's hand and begin to pray, "Father God. We are poor and simple people who carry terrible burdens. The three of us done sinful things that are contrary to your Holy Word. We need your help and forgiveness if we are gonna' carry on. I want to say my thanks for you getting my Nina away from Satan. Today, he tried to take her down to his awful place. We know you sent your Angels to help us. We is thankin' you right now and I am asking for your protection 'cause Satan ain't done with us. There is someone else watching and waiting to do harm to us. Please, dear Father in Heaven, we need you. I ask all of these things in Your Holy Name. Amen."

When Linnie finished, Hank walked over and gave Linnie a hug and kissed her on the cheek. She was surprised at his gentleness and show of affection. She looked up at him and said, "Oh Hank. Where would we be if you and Gator weren't here?" Hank answered, "Well Linnie, me and Gator are here and we ain't gonna' leave, not until you say so." He held Linnie closer and said, "Linnie, today when I thought of you getting hurt, I felt something I haven't felt in many years. I need to tell you that you have stolen my heart. Do you think you could ever love someone like me. I ain't got much to offer; just my love and protection. Is that good enough?"

Linnie smiled, and gave him a kiss right on the mouth. She said, "Hank. I have been waitin' for someone like you for a long, long time." Hank kneeled down beside her and took her hand, "Linnie. Would you do me the honor of bein' my bride?" Linnie giggled, "Oh Hank. Yes." Nina was watching but wasn't really understanding what was happening. Her head wasn't fully clear and her thoughts were slow to process the conversation.

Linnie saw the confused look in her eyes, she lovingly said, "Nina. Hank wants to stay with us forever to keep us safe. What do you think? Is it a good idea?" Nina seemed to comprehend what she asked. She nodded yes and lovingly touched Linnie's cheek. She responded in a weak and quiet voice, "Yes, Linnie." Linnie took Nina's hand and kissed it and began to laugh and cry at the same time. With a joyous voice she said, "I got a family again. Thank you Jesus for this here miracle."

That day was filled with many miracles. God honored Linnie's prayers and the Cajun was crushed by the hand of God. God also chose to give all of them a special gift, the restoration of their broken and lost lives. It was the first step toward the three to heal and start a new life. During their previous lives, they suffered incredible pain and were separated from God. Their lives had been torn apart from tragic losses that cut deep wounds in their hearts. Yes, God delivered several miracles that day because He is faithful, His grace is free and His love is immeasurable.

That day, Ornella's slayer lost his life and would never kill again. Also, Nina broke free from her stupor. As a result, a new family was birthed and God's glory and majesty was revealed. It was an amazing day because when the morning sun broke through the thick fog, it was the beginning of a wonderfully new day. The blackness of Satan was pierced with the glorious Light of God. His life-giving light held promise for the three for a happy and blessed future.

Linnie was grateful God freed Nina from Satan's prison but she was still burdened for her. Her heart was troubled and she faithfully prayed that Nina would give up her clients. As often as she could, she spoke to Nina about doing so. Nina never gave her a definite answer and Linnie became deeply worried. She shared her concern with Hank. As they sat at the kitchen table he said, "Why don't you ask your preacher to stop by and talk to us 'bout getting married? When he is here, it might be a good notion to ask if he would chat with Nina, too."

Linnie answered, "That might be the way to do it. I ain't gettin' no place with her. She don't give me a yes or no." The next Sunday at church, Linnie told the preacher that Hank wanted to get married. She didn't forget to mention her worries about Nina. He agreed to stop by. A few days after Linnie talked to him, he knocked on the door. Hank welcomed him with a warm and firm manly handshake and offered

him a place at the kitchen table. All four were
there and they sat at the well-worn kitchen table.
They shared coffee and an apple pie purchased
from the local bakery. There was small talk for a
few minutes, then the preacher spoke to Hank
and Linnie about getting married.

He asked a lot of questions and one was
about them living together. Hank answered
without hesitation, "If you are askin' if we are
livin' in sin and having relations, well we ain't. I
stay in the shed when night comes. I slept in the
house just when Nina was sick in the head. Uh,
no disrespect Nina. But, when she woke up, I
went straight away to the shed where I belong."
The preacher smiled and answered, "That is the
answer I was wanting. I can't perform a marriage
ceremony if it doesn't honor God. Now that you
assured me you both respect God and his
precepts, I will gladly perform the ceremony.
When do you want to schedule it?" He pulled
out a worn and well-used pocket calendar.

He put his stub of a pencil in his mouth as if
wetting it would make it write better. That was a
habit of his and one he couldn't break. Hank said,
"We are ready any time after we get the license.
Can we get married in the church?" The
preacher said he approved, but he asked if he
could counsel them first. Linnie and Hank

agreed to the counseling. They both agreed it was a good idea since both had suffered previous marriage failures.

He asked, "Do you want the church folks to be there? They would be honored to attend your special day. The church ladies would love to make a celebration meal for the new bride and groom. Our choir director can play the piano and his wife can sing. We can make it a beautiful wedding that you two deserve. There won't be a cost. Linnie has been so good to the women who visit the church that we want to give her a gift of love." Linnie smiled and turned to Hank, he said, "I want my Linnie to have the best."

The preacher turned to face Nina. He directed his next question to her, "Did you know Linnie helps the women who come to church; the ones from the streets. They are lost souls who live by selling their bodies for drug money or alcohol or anything they need to live. Linnie prays for them and tells them that God loves them. She is our prayer warrior and we are blessed to have her." Nina's face turned dark red, her bottom lip drooped and quivered.

Her eyes filled with large tears that flowed down her face. The preacher touched her shoulder, "Nina. I want to pray for you, right

128

now. Linnie has been doing it for a long time. I want to do my part to help you break free of Satan's hold on your life. Only God can break the chains that bound you to Satan. May I be part of asking God do that for you? God loves you with an incredible love that you deserve to receive." Nina put her head into her hands, then dropped her head and shoulders to the table. She began to shake as she sobbed and moaned.

The preacher leaned over and put his strong arms around her shoulders. He quoted, Psalm 86:5, "For thou, Lord, art good, and ready to forgive; And plenteous in mercy unto all them that call upon thee." He opened his Bible to a page marked with a torn piece of paper and read from it, Isaiah 43:25, "I, even I, am he that blotteth out thy transgressions for mine own sake, and will not remember thy sins." He opened it to another marked passage and read from 1st John 1:9, "If we confess our sins, he is faithful and just to forgive us sins, and to cleanse us from all unrighteousness,"

He continued, "Nina. Don't run from God. He is waiting for you to turn around and take His hand so He can help you. Just ask Him, and He will blot out your past sin from your life. His forgiveness and love are free because His Son, Jesus, gave His life so that we can be saved and be adopted as His children." Nina slowly raised her head as she mumbled, "I know. When I was sick I heard him talking to me. Let me tell you what happened." The preacher looked surprised and eager to hear her story. She said, "Linnie. Could you please give me a glass of cool water to clear my throat?" Linnie enthusiastically granted her request and as Nina drank it, she seemed calmed and controlled.

She began with, "First of all, Linnie, I couldn't give you an answer about my men friends. My boss expected me to keep his customers happy. If I was to up and quit, I could lose my job and you know no one else in this town would hire a sinful woman like me. I knew I was ready to change; but my head was full of other people talking to me at the same time. I think when you hear my dream you will understand. This is what I dreamed all the days I was froze up in fear." Her voice was soft, but firm and as she shared what was buried in her memory. She began to slowly talk as her eyes were closed and she was seeing something replay before them.

She began her story, "I came home sick in the head, after meeting my last client. That night I learned that while he was vacationing in the swamps, he met my brothers. Not knowing who they were, he told them that a woman he knew was raised in the swamps. As soon as he said that I felt strange, like something or someone was choking me. I left right away saying I was getting sick and needed to go home. My legs were so wobbly I could hardly walk to the bus stop. All the way home, I felt like I was being followed by something evil. When I got home, all I wanted to do was look out the window to see if my brothers were watching the house. Then, I drifted off to sleep or something. I can't describe exactly what it was. Right off I began to dream."

She paused for a moment, then continued, "I think that was when I went out of my head; you know, I couldn't talk or move. I was living in another world. In it, I kept running and running. I ran so much I couldn't catch my breath. It seemed as if I had been running for years and years. I think I was running to escape something really mean and awful that hovered over me and watched me. Then, I saw a stranger. He waived at me and knew my name."

She continued, "The stranger said, 'Nina, turn around, you are running the wrong way.' I ignored them. I started to run again. As I ran, I saw a lot of strangers. All told me the same thing. After what seemed like ages; I saw my mama waiving at me. She stopped me and took

131

my hand, she said, 'Nina. Turn around now before it is too late.' I broke away from her and kept running. Finally, I fell on my knees. So tired I couldn't stand up.'"

She asked for more water, drank the entire glass in one gulp and started again, "When I looked around, I was in this house. My hands and feet were bloody and sore and I couldn't use my legs. I crawled to the bathroom. I pulled myself up to the sink and held onto it to keep from falling. I looked in the mirror. What I saw looking back at me was just awful. I saw a wrinkled, toothless old lady staring at me. I couldn't believe my eyes; it was me. I crumpled onto the floor and screamed and cried. I shook my fist at God and the whole world. I was mad at everyone and I blamed everyone except myself for what I had become. Then God said something."

In a more confident voice she said, "It wasn't really a voice, just a thought. I knew it was God. I truly believe He was talking to me. This is what I heard, 'Nina, I love you. To me you are my beautiful daughter. Let me hold you and tell you how much I love you, because at this very minute I have never loved you more.' Then there was a loud bang or pop from something close by. I heard police sirens. I heard people talking and I felt Linnie standing beside me. That was when I woke up.'"

She took a deep breath and said, "I am not finished, there is more. Since my dream, God and other voices keep speaking to me. Linnie, when you try to talk to me, I hear the other voices, too. They are telling me God will protect me because I am His beautiful daughter. Oh preacher, I am so confused. My head is filled with lots of folks I don't know talking to me. Sometimes I think I am going crazy. You know, just plain out of my head cause I can't break free of all them voices."

She took a deep breath before continuing, "At night, when I am asleep, is when I find peace. I dream about beautiful angels and music that must be from heaven. The sounds are not anything I have heard before. I feel as if I am being lifted up and comforted and filled with something new and wonderful. I don't want to wake up. I keep wanting to go back. I don't know how to explain it. Is that what Heaven is like. You know, where everybody is nice and the air is filled with beautiful music and feelings of love?"

After Nina finished, she was no longer crying. Her face had a luminous glow and her eyes were clear and bright. She looked different. It was amazing to see the transformation. The three of them gazed at her in astonishment. They knew they had witnessed something incredible. The old Nina was gone. The new Nina was sitting at the table waiting for an answer. There was a short moment of still silence, then the preacher responded. He seemed to be as surprised as everyone was, "Nina. While you were dreaming did you ask Jesus to forgive your sins?"

She answered, "Yes. As soon as I came around after I heard the shot. I told Jesus that if I was alive, to please forgive me for my terrible life. I told Jesus I needed Him more than anything. I asked Him to fill me with His love and protection. Do you think He heard me?" The preacher replied, "Without a doubt, Jesus heard and you have been fully forgiven." Nina said, "You know, since then I feel different and I sense that someone loves me. Do you know who it is?"

He answered, "The Holy Ghost is our counselor and comforter that Jesus gave us after he went back to Heaven. It is nourishing your empty soul with God's love. You are being filled with His love. I also believe it is talking to you and trying to help you. I have never heard a testimony like yours. To help you understand your new life and journey with Christ, my wife and I would be honored to disciple you. It is time to no longer be confused or afraid. Nina, tonight you finally turned around and quit chasing Satan. God was right beside you all the time calling out to you. When you were staring out the window, you met Angels who tried to help you see God. They were telling you that God wanted to help you because you are His child." After that night, Hank took it upon himself to help Nina get a decent job after she quit the bar. Her transition was beautiful; no longer was she running and living in fear.

God was still watching over her and one night he sent her a dream. First thing the next morning she shared the dream with Linnie and Hank. She said, "Last night, while I was asleep I felt something or someone watching me. Suddenly, a person was standing at the foot of my bed. I don't know if I was awake or still dreaming. The person said, 'Be vigilant. Seek the Lord thy God for protection. Satan, the devil and destroyer is on the prowl. Three of his henchmen are watching and waiting for a time to strike.'" Immediately after she told them, she knew it was a warning about her three brothers. She told Linnie and Hank she thought it was an angel warning them of danger.

Fearing for their safety, the three decided to talk to the police. Once there, the police intently listened to Nina as she shared the evilness she experienced while living with her brothers. Nina was shocked when the police told her that all three brothers were outside of town, in the old adobe shack. The police said that they had just met them. They became aware of them that morning as they searched the Cajun's shack. As they rummaged through the Cajun's trash, they heard a truck engine back-firing. It seemed to be nearby and close to the abandoned adobe rest stop. One deputy set out on foot to investigate the noise. As he walked toward the sound, he stopped dead in his tracks when he saw what was stored outside. He spied gasoline cans and boxes of dynamite. His training told him to back off and tell the other deputies what he saw.

He returned and shared what he discovered. They decided to leave the Cajun's shack to investigate. Not wanting to arouse whoever was inside and potentially dangerous, they quietly walked toward the shack with guns drawn. One deputy remained outside while two deputies leaned close to the door. They were able to overhear men inside brag about their guns and explosives. Knowing they were listening to a what could be a deadly encounter, they kicked open the door with pistols pointed at the brothers.

Seeing the deputies with weapons drawn, the brothers knew they had no time to grab their guns. The three hit the floor. They yelled, "We ain't carrying no firearms. Don't shoot." The deputies cautiously entered the shack, ready to shoot if any made a threatening move. They walked in to see three shaking, dirty-smelly cowards laying on their stomachs. The brothers' hands were trembling and beads of sweat covered their dirty faces. Realizing they were caught, their alcohol-laced bravado was replaced with a pitiful display of cowardice.

They were immediately handcuffed to chairs so the deputies were safe to examine the place. Several rifles, boxes of ammunition, more dynamite, and gasoline cans were discovered. The dynamite was immediately confiscated. Then, they began to question the brothers. The brothers answered that they were there to hunt. They said the dynamite was already in the shack and they didn't know how to get rid of it.

Knowing they were lying, the deputies warned them to get out of town. They said they knew they were up to no good and it wasn't safe for them to hang around these parts. One deputy called them deadbeats and crooks. Taking offense, one brother lurched for the deputy but he was still handcuffed to a chair. He tumbled with the chair on top of him. The deputy pulled him over and said, "Listen, and listen good. You scum bags better start packing up and leaving before sunset. You got no business here and we don't cotton to you hanging around."

After the deputies left, the brothers agreed it was time to show everyone in that no-good town who was boss. Yes, that very evening, not only would Nina be kidnapped and tortured and left to die, but the small town would explode and go up in flames. The plan was to drive into town during the dark of night. They would store the Molotov cocktails in the bed of the truck. Once in town, one brother would move to the back. As the truck raced through the streets, he would light up the town with deadly cocktails and the other two would spray it with gunfire. All three agreed it was a great plan and they were ready to put it into action.

Not satisfied with killing animals in the swamps, they had yearned for years to be able commit the ultimate crime. Their wicked minds desired to murder a multitude of victims at one time. The remainder of that day, the three brothers engrossed themselves in their blueprint for terror. They became energized and insanely embolden as they imagined Nina's screams for mercy from the terror they were to inflict. The three agreed that her death would be delayed so she could watch them torch the town. After they finished their horrible attack on the town, Nina would be thrown out of truck as they sped out of town.

Nina, God has a plan for the Old Oak Tree to defeat your enemy; Satan, the father of lies.

"And he answered and spake unto those that stood before him, saying, Take away the filthy garments from him. And unto him he said, Behold, I have caused thine iniquity to pass from thee, and I will clothe thee with change of raiment."
(Zechariah 3:4 KJV)

Chapter 8

God's Plan is Perfect

That evening, the brothers were anxious to implement their deadly plan. They were unaware the deputies had their own plan. It was heavily weighted in their favor; only two roads connected the brothers to the town. The deputies had set up two roadblocks and were ready and waiting. Both roads had deputies waiting behind wooden barriers. There were plenty of men positioned, ready to stop the brothers. Ten heavily-armed men, at each intersection, were prepared to stop them. All vehicles, including farm trucks, were humming and drivers were positioned for a potential chase. Late that evening, almost midnight, the three brothers, drove their truck toward town.

It didn't take long for the group at the roadblock to know the brothers were on the move. The sound of a misfiring truck was heard heading toward the northern roadblock. Deputies and volunteers crouched behind their vehicles and the wooden barricade. Their guns were loaded and cocked, ready to fire. They intently waited. At a one-mile intersection the noisy truck, loaded with deadly cargo turned toward them. In a few seconds, two yellow headlights were seen driving straight toward the roadblock. It was headed at a fairly fast pace and was coming straight on; right into the line of fire. Two tough and weathered farmers yelled, "Those fools don't know what is waitin' for them." That was the absolute truth. What happened next was incredible.

When the truck was less than a quarter mile away, it began to slow. Then it stopped. The brothers jumped out of the truck and started firing at the barricade. Since the brothers were full of whiskey and other hard liquor, their aim wasn't too good. They managed to shoot up the surrounding orchards and scare off the crows and pigeons that were settled in the trees for the night. Hearing the birds overhead flying and screeching, the men behind the barricade laughed.

The brother's feeble attempt to take them down failed in a shower of bird feathers and dust. Taking advantage of the break and the poor aim of the brothers, one man raised a bullhorn and yelled, "Ya' got no chance of escapin', ya' no counts. We got ya' surrounded on all roads. Give up before we come an git ya', ya' lousy shots. All you killed was a few birds sitting in the trees."

With that said, the men behind the barricade hooted and slapped each other on the back. Enraged, the three brothers clearly heard them mocking them as they jumped back into the truck. Angry and humiliated, they turned their rickety truck around in a flash of dust and gravel. Seeing their retreat, the barricade of men emptied in a flash and all were right on their tail. The race was on. While driving, one deputy said, "Those varmints will turn toward their hideout. Hey, git on the radio and tell the other group to get going to block them." In a few seconds, the southern barricade was speeding toward Old Telegraph Road.

As the three brothers raced back to their shack, they turned on Old Telegraph Road. The new plan was to hold up in the shack and make a standoff. Once there, they would hold up in the adobe shack and put up a fierce fight. Even if they didn't win, they figured they would make a good killing that night. In their deranged minds, they were elated about the ensuing battle.

As they raced their junked-out truck toward their hideout, they yelled and swigged their hard liquor. They were so drunk their brains were numbed. All they could think about was the promise of the kill and savor of freshly spewed blood flowing in abundance. As they drove and

143

drank, their pitiful excuse of a vehicle belched swirling black smoke. If it had been daylight, an onlooker would have seen the face of Satan in it.

The brother driving the truck rammed the gas pedal down in a feeble attempt to outrun the deputies. Miraculously, he felt the truck gain speed. The three looked up and saw several more headlights heading toward them. They realized they were headed toward a large group of vehicles. Panic set in; they weren't going to make it to the shack. Behind them was the enemy and more were barreling toward them. The brother driving said, "Let's keep going and crash right through them. When they see we ain't backin' down, those yellow-bellied cops will pull over." That sounded like a sure-fire plan. What they didn't know was that the old oak tree, the town sentinel, was waiting for them.

As all this was happening, the old oak tree stood silently and watched and waited. It stood firm and strong while its branches hung over the road. Somehow, the brothers' truck picked up more speed. It had quit backfiring and seemed to glide over the road. It was as if something unseen had given it a resurgence of power. Within a few yards of the old oak tree, the truck became airborne. The three brothers yelled in delight; free from the pavement they felt as if they were flying.

For the second time in the history of the town, the old oak tree took a major hit. The airborne truck slammed into its thick and sturdy trunk. On impact it immediately burst into flames. Within seconds the Molotov cocktails in the back of the truck exploded in a fury of violently loud explosions. The gas tank followed and the truck became a burning inferno. Both groups of pursuers slammed to a stop.

Dirt, dust and gravel scattered everywhere. The deputies and men town folk jumped out of their vehicles. As they ran they used their arms to shield them from the onslaught of flying debris. The night air was eerily silent as no screams were heard from the brothers. The only sound was the roaring of the intensely hot fire. Then, a loud whoosh of wind fed the scorching flames. Red hot flames climbed upward into the night air and reared to almost a hundred feet. It was a flame that could be seen for miles. After the air cleared a bit, they took off their hats, ran their fingers through their hair (if they had some) and stared at the grisly fire.

The inferno was so intense, the men watching felt their skin begin to burn from the searing heat.

145

They took shelter behind their vehicles in fear that another explosion would send shrapnel to rip through their bodies. In dead silence, they watched as the truck and its occupants burned in the blazing fire. One onlooker said, "This ain't no regular fire. This is fire straight from hell. Nobody, no way, is gonna' live through that. We might never know what is the truck and what is the person after it stops. Lord have mercy on them three wayward souls."

It took several days for the molten truck to cool enough so it could be pulled off and taken to the dump. Even when it was separated from the tree trunk, parts of it glowed red and was still smoldering. Once totally separated from the tree, it was loaded on a flatbed truck and hauled away to the local grave yard for vehicles. Through all of this, the old oak tree stood strong.

Its trunk was black but barely damaged. The men who hauled off the truck were awestruck that the tree didn't fall over or completely burn. Some said it was an omen for evil doers to stay away from Old Telegraph Road. Some said the old oak tree was the protector that took care of those who tried to harm their town. Maybe they were right.

Word got out about the accident and people from all around came to take pictures of the tree and the mangled, melted truck. So many people came that the junk yard owner put up a sign that read, "This here is the truck that holds the bodies of 3 varmints who meant to do our town harm." He also put up a sign that said, "Photos with the truck - $3.00 per car load." He made good money for several years from those signs. Town folks said, "Well, those three varmints were good for something. They helped the junk yard owner get enough money for a new set of teeth."

Not everyone was attracted to the scene of the wreck, there were some that chose to stay away. Nina, Hank and Linnie were three of them. They didn't visit the junkyard for several years. Nina couldn't face seeing the blackened coffin of her brothers. She said it would bring back all the bad memories of when they abused her as a child. Her decision to avoid her brother's final resting place was a good one. When she did choose to visit the mangled coffin of her brothers, Satan and his demons were waiting for her.

Clothed with Clean Garments

After the death of her brothers, Nina regularly attended Linnie's church. A few months later, during church service, the preacher spoke on

Zechariah 3:4. "And he answered and spake unto those that stood before him, saying, Take away the filthy garments from him. And unto him he said, Behold, I have caused thine iniquity to pass from thee, and I will clothe thee with change of raiment."

The people of Jerusalem had sinned and turned away from God. The preacher said sin makes us dirty or unclean before God because God is pure and sinless. He finished by saying, "When we are forgiven of our sins, God clothes us in clean, white garments." Nina felt as if the preacher was directly speaking to her. Something stirred inside her soul and she began to understand that she was finally free of her past.

That day, she felt a heavy weight leave her. She realized she would no longer carry the burden of shame for her sins. For once, Nina was ready to completely stop running. That was when she fully accepted His free gift of forgiveness and salvation. Any doubt she carried before was gone. She knew she was completely forgiven and was ready to move forward with her new life. It would be a life that she had never dreamed of; a life designed by God for her. One that God had been wanting to give her for many years.

During those months, she transitioned from a woman hiding from her past to a woman living in the Light of God. She realized her past was no longer important because Christ had deleted it, forever. The old Nina no longer existed. Now, what was important was her future. For once in her life actually looked forward to her future. It would be one that promised peace, love and hope. The chains that Satan had bound her with were gone; broken by God because Linnie was given a heavenly commission to guide her.

Linnie often read two verses to Nina when she became discouraged. The first was, Ephesians 5;14, "Wherefore he saith, Awake thou that sleepest, and arise from the dead, and Christ shall give thee light." The second was, Galatians 2:20, "I am crucified with Christ: nevertheless I live; yet not I, but Christ liveth in me: and the life which I now live in the flesh I live by the faith of the Son of God, who loved me, and gave himself for me."

One day while visiting with Linnie she shared, "When I feel sad and lost, I recall these Holy Words and I am lifted up. It makes my heart sing. They are medicine to my soul and I need them with me all the time." As the days and years passed, the two became closer, almost as if they were truly mother and daughter. Nina's change and openness to intimacy with God filled a deep and painful void in both their hearts. Hank saw the new intimacy between Nina and Linnie. It convinced him to start attending church with them. After all, he thought, he and Linnie had been married in it and the people were kind and friendly.

Their wedding had been perfect. Linnie wore a pale blue suit with white flowers in her hair and a matching bouquet. Hank wore an ironed and starched white shirt with dark gray dress pants. Nina wore a light yellow dress with blue and white flowers embroidered around the neck and the bottom of the skirt. The church people did everything the preacher said they would; the day was perfect. After the wedding reception, all three walked home to their small house. The day before the wedding, Nina moved into Hank's small house. It was Nina who chose to move out because she finally felt safe living alone.

Over the years, Hank continued to work on the Nina's little house until it resembled a pretty cottage. He planted flowers in the front and put green shutters around the windows. He painted it white and added a small modern kitchen and bath. Nina was comfortable in the little house and felt as if she had her own home. Not to be separated from Nina, Gator took up residence in the tiny cottage. He remained her protector until he died. Hank buried him in the back yard and put rocks on top of his grave. He made a cross for Gator's grave and engraved the words, "Gator – Nina's Angel."

Nina grew strong and healthy as she became closer to the Lord. She began to reach out to women who were scared, just as she had been. Over time, Linnie and Nina became well known in town as godly women who helped the unfortunate and poor of the town. If a business owner saw someone walking the streets, hungry and lost, he sent them to their church. It was the two of them who knew how to talk to lost souls. They spoke their language and understood their needs and inner fears. Clearly, God was using the two women's previous lives to prepare them for their ministry. Over the years, many souls were saved and lives were spared the tragedy that Ornella suffered.

Many Years Later

The days, weeks, months and years rapidly passed. To Nina, it seemed as if only a few years had passed and somehow she realized she was close to forty years old. Nina didn't feel old and was still a very comely woman. She was happy and her new life gave her face a beautiful glow.

Her life was full, peaceful and for once, she believed she was helping people. She gave no thought to falling in love and getting married. Her life in Christ with her friends and God's love were all she needed. Then something unexpected happened, one evening before church service a man came to church.

He was tall and slim and had curly black hair. He was freshly shaven and looked as if his hair was recently cut. His clothes were clean, but not new. He wore worn and scuffed work boots that were polished and shiny. It was obvious he was a working man. From his appearance, it was evident he took time to be presentable and proper in church. Immediately, Nina noticed him but turned her back to him. She didn't want him to think she was flirting. Men had not been a part of her life for several years and she wasn't interested in meeting one. Not now; not when things were going so smoothly. Her past experience with men was shameful and she didn't believe she could ever find a man to love her.

Even though her first response was to ignore him, she noticed he had a pleasant face. She was also impressed that he took off his hat when he entered church. Linnie saw Nina glancing at him, she said, "Nina. Who is that man? I don't recall seeing him before?" Nina looked at her and shrugged her shoulders. Linnie said, "Church ain't started yet. Why don't you walk back there and welcome him?" Nina, surprised at her request firmly answered, "No, I won't do it. Hank, why don't you go introduce yourself to him?"

Not listening to what the two women had been saying, Hank said, "What? Who? What are you two wanting me to do?" Linnie leaned toward him and said, "Hank. Open your eyes. There is a man sitting in the back row. I don't remember him being here before. Go and welcome him, proper like." Hank mumbled, "Alright. I will." He stood up, excused himself and walked toward the stranger. He held out his hand to the man and said, "Let me welcome you to our church. I am Hank. Who might you be?"

Nina could hear their conversation but she didn't turn around. She kept her face forward as she strained to listen to what was said. The man stood up. He was head and shoulders taller than Hank. Hank said, "If you ain't a tall drink of water." The man smiled and answered in a deep voice, "Glad to meet you, Hank." He extended his hand to Hank and both men shook hands. "I am Homer Judkin. I am here working on the machines at the packing sheds. I am staying with my brother, a few streets over." Hank said, "Well, we are glad you are here. We hope you enjoy the service." Homer said his thanks and returned to his seat. That was when Hank noticed a guitar case next to him. Hank said, "Do you play that thing?" Homer answered, "I guess some folks think I can. I sing a bit too. When I am home, I sing and play for my church."

That night, Homer played his guitar and sang. He had a deep, clear voice that filled the small church. Nina tried to keep from watching him; she pretended to be reading her Bible while he sang. After church, she avoided talking to him as she exited out the back of the church. Her past years of poor experiences with men made her uncomfortable talking to them. Over the next few weeks, Homer continued to attend church and to sing and play his guitar. Each time Nina saw him, she found a way to evade him. One time before church started, he walked directly toward Nina. She looked around hoping to find a way to escape. Homer was determined to not let her get away. He walked up to her and asked if he could sit beside her. Nina, embarrassed didn't quite know how to answer him.

She turned to Linnie and asked, "Do you mind?" Linnie muffled a laugh and answered, "Nina. You are a grown woman. Make up your own mind. Me and Hank would like it, but he didn't ask us." Linnie's response made her blush. She instinctively grabbed her neck. It was warm and was turning bright red. She couldn't remember the last time she had blushed. Linnie gave her a sideways glance and said, "Nina, answer the man. He is standing here and you are ignoring him. Don't be impolite. You know that it ain't right for a Christian woman to be rude." Homer spoke up, "Nina. Speak up if you think I am being too forward."

Nina moved her hand from her neck and choked out her answer, "Homer. No man has asked to sit by me, ever. Not in church, not anyplace. I was surprised to be asked. Of course, all three of us would be pleased if you would join us." Homer took her arm with one hand as he carried his guitar in the other. He walked her to the row where Hank, Linnie and she always set. He didn't sit until both Nina and Linnie were properly seated. He looked at Hank and winked as he took his seat. Oddly, Nina felt at ease sitting next to Homer. Her previous life with men varied from tragic abuse to degrading sex with clients. With Homer sitting beside her, she began to sense something new and different growing inside her heart.

155

After that Sunday, sitting beside Homer in church was a normal routine. The two were together every Sunday morning and evening, and during Wednesday evening Bible study. Anytime the church doors were open, she and Homer were together. She admitted to Linnie that being close to Homer felt natural and she was relaxed in his presence. It wasn't long until Linnie invited Homer to Sunday dinner at their small home. The meals were simple, but Homer didn't complain. Nina noticed he was good at keeping a conversation going.

He brightened their Sunday dinners. He had an excellent knowledge of the Bible and enjoyed talking about it. He shared that his parents lived in northern California. His father, Herbert, grew Christmas trees and his mother, Annette, made quilts, jam and homemade candies. They sold Christmas trees during the holidays as well as the items his mother made. His mother also made quilts for the local shop and gave quilting lessons during the off season.

Homer was the mechanic on the family farm and knew how to repair and rebuild almost any type of farm equipment. He shared that his mechanical skills brought him to Nina's small town. The local packing sheds had problems keeping a machine repairman; most were drifters and drank too much. Homer's brother, Arnold, recommended him to the farmer who owned the sheds. Arnold sent for him and as soon as the farmer interviewed Homer, he hired him. They hit it off immediately. Within a short time, it looked as if the farmer would offer him a fulltime job. One day at Sunday dinner, Homer said, "He keeps asking me if I like the town and if I would consider settling down here. I told him I like it just fine." When Nina heard that she could feel her heartbeat in her throat. Could it be she was falling in love for the first time in her life?

Nina, God desires to shower you with love,
even one you never expected.

*"Blessed [are] they that mourn: for
they shall be comforted."*
(Matthew 5:4 KJV)

Chapter 9

HOMER

Homer was raised on a farm in northern California. As a young child, he showed a talent for fixing things. He enjoyed taking things apart and then trying to figure out how to put them back together. His inquisitive mind carried into school where he was a good student; mathematics were his strength. He also participated in sports, but music captured his heart. He attempted to play several instruments and eventually settled on the guitar. After his voice changed from falsetto to bass, about the age of fourteen or fifteen, he discovered his true singing voice, a beautiful deep baritone.

While attending high school he sang in the choir. During church he played his guitar and often sang solos. Throughout his high school years he grew into a fine young man who excelled in academics and sports. In his small school he became well-known and popular. Less than a thousand students attended his school. Most of the students came from middle-class families. Many residents were small-business owners or farmers who raised table crops or managed fruit orchards. Crisp, juicy Macintosh apples were the main crop. The cold winters and warm summers were perfect for growing them.

Some of the farms grew berries of all kinds, including cranberries. There was ample rain to water all the farms and annual harvests were usually good. Seldom was there a drought because they were located far enough north to share Oregon's incredible yearly rainfall. The crops grown within the region provided ample produce for nearby stores that showcased local homemade jams, jellies and baked goods.

The town was small and intimate and displayed locally-owned businesses. They sold a variety of local artisan creations. The shops provided a rich resource for out-of-town visitors seeking to purchase unique, handmade items. As a result, holidays were busy times for local merchants. Homer's family Christmas tree farm was one of the holiday favorites.

While growing up on the family farm, Homer developed his skills for repairing machines of all types. He could repair or rebuild small engines, power tools, tractors and harvesting equipment. It was this skill that got the attention of a local business; a tractor and farm equipment business. When Homer finished high school, he was offered a position. He worked at the business with the agreement that he could continue his education at the resident college. The owner knew he had a valuable employee, so Homer was given a flexible schedule so he could continue his education. He worked in the afternoon and evenings after his day classes ended. It was a good arrangement and Homer excelled in his classes and at work.

The majority of the college courses were in the campus main building; a two-story older red-brick structure. There was an elevator but most students used the stairs. Between classes the stairs were crowded and often rushing students bumped into each other. Students didn't want to be late to class because some professors would lock the doors as soon as the second bell rang.

Those who were late were locked out and counted absent. Only three absences were allowed. After three, students would be dropped from the class. If dropped they had to repeat the class. Not wanting to repeat a class and delay graduation, students didn't dally on the stairways. As a result, students who wanted to flirt or visit delayed their social interests until lunch or after their last class.

It was on those stairs that Homer met his future wife. One cold winter day, Homer was hurrying up the stairway. He stopped to see a pretty blond girl who had dropped her books and binder. He noticed she was struggling to pick up her scattered items. Homer being the gentleman he was, stopped to help her. She attempted to discourage him because she knew he would be late for class. Homer wasn't one to give up, he stayed with her until everything was in her hands. When finished she gave him a quick thank you and ran to class. The second bell rang before both got to their classroom doors. Both were locked out. Homer was at one end of the long hallway and she was at the other end.

Homer looked toward her and said, "Well. I guess we have about forty-five minutes to get to know each other." When she heard him she answered, "Okay. Sounds like a plan. Are you coming my way or do I need to walk your way?" Homer laughed and answered, "I am a gentleman so I will walk your way." She leaned her shoulder against the wall and watched him walk toward her. She hadn't noticed before, but he was tall and rather handsome. He had dark hair and his long arms were muscular. She thought to herself, "Wow. I must be getting blind. He is quite an eye full." As Homer walked toward her, he noticed she was slim and had shiny blond hair. He also observed that her tight skirt and sweater showed off her curvy figure. He thought that this is my lucky day. He pondered, "I wonder how I missed her? She doesn't look familiar. I don't think she went to my high school or I would have noticed her. Guess I have a few minutes to impress her."

Homer was the first to open conversation. He said, "Where is your next class?" She replied, "This is my last class. I go to work right after. Oh man, I hate missing it. They are reviewing for the mid-term exam." Homer replied with a smile and air of confidence, "This is my last class, too. I got to go to work today. Sounds like we are on the same schedule. What do you say we get a snack in the cafeteria? Oh, what class are you missing?" She answered, pleased to see that he was more handsome than she first thought, "Oh, it's Psych 105. My professor, Mr. Nelson, is really tough."

Homer took her arm and said, "Well. This is your lucky day. I passed his class last semester. You know, he never changes his tests. He just mixes up the questions each year. I can help you study cause I got an A." She smiled and said, "By the way, my name is Abigail. What's yours?" He answered, "Most folks call me Homer. But I will answer to anything when food is in the offering." They both laughed and headed for the warmth of the cafeteria.

That was the beginning of their courtship. Abigail liked Homer from their first meeting on the college stairway. Even though she asked him to not help her, she was happy he did. That first day when he was carefully gathering her scattered papers and books, she was thinking he must be a caring and mannerly young man. During their courtship, she discovered he was just as she thought when she first met him. As for Homer, he fell head-over-heels in love, almost immediately.

As they got acquainted he learned he was right, she hadn't gone to his high school. During the summer after graduation, she and her family moved from Oregon to his small town. They had relocated because her father got a job as the local postmaster and her mother was to work at a local quilt shop. Homer and Abigail were married almost two years after they graduated from college. They were married in the spring when the surrounding orchards were in full bloom.

It was a small traditional wedding with Homer and Abigail's family in attendance and a few close friends. There was a reception at the church with food and music. Homer played and sang, *Can't Help Falling in Love With You.*[ix] The newly married couple honeymooned for ten days in Washington. They traveled to the San Juan

164

Islands and stayed at a bed and breakfast on Friday Harbor. The weather was sunny as they walked around the small town. During the ride on the ferry back to the mainland, they saw dolphins and whales swimming in the deep blue ocean water. It was a wonderful honeymoon and the young couple vowed they would return every anniversary.

After the honeymoon, both parents gave them a warm homecoming in the couple's new home. It was a small house not far from the family tree farm. Homer was given a fulltime position to work at the farm machinery company. During the Christmas holidays he took a short vacation to help with the family tree farm. Before long, Abigail left her job to help Homer's mother start a small quilt and jam shop located on the farm. It was a happy time for both of them and after six months, Abigail discovered she was pregnant.

Everyone was elated with the news of a first grandchild. The pregnancy was uneventful and Abigail glowed during the months she carried their precious baby. She was in good health and her doctor assured everyone that both mother and child were doing well. They prepared the nursery for the new arrival as they impatiently waited for her due date. No one anticipated the unexpected tragedy that awaited them.

The due date came and no labor pains or baby arrived. The doctor said not to worry, it wasn't unusual for the first baby to be a few days or even a week or so late. After two weeks, Abigail became troubled and she pressed the doctor for an answer during her exam. After the exam, the doctor said the baby was getting big and if she wanted, he would induce labor the next morning. Overdue and uncomfortable, Abigail eagerly agreed to the procedure to get her labor started. She shared the decision with Homer and both agreed it was a good idea. Very early the next morning they arrived at the small hospital.

Abigail was admitted to the hospital labor and delivery wing. It was painted with soft colors and the walls were decorated with watercolor prints of flowers and peaceful scenes. Once she was examined and settled into the labor room, the doctor started her intravenous infusion that delivered a mixture similar to the natural hormone that produces labor. Homer was with her as her labor began. After several hours of painful labor, Abigail began to bleed. The nurse immediately called the doctor. He was napping in the staff rest area ready to deliver her baby at a moment's notice. The bleeding was abnormal and he asked Homer to step into the waiting room and to call both of their parents.

Homer made the call with a feeling of overwhelming trepidation. He tried to be calm as he explained something wasn't right and that Abigail was bleeding. It didn't take long until all four parents arrived. They came with faces gripped in fear. Homer's father took control and asked everyone to pray for Abigail and the new grandchild. As they were praying, the doctor came into the room. He said, "I am so sorry to tell you that we have a serious problem. The baby is in stress and Abigail has started to hemorrhage. I am having her immediately moved to surgery. We will do what we can to save the baby and Abigail." When he finished, he wiped his sweaty forehead with his hand and said, "Please keep praying. Don't stop. We need all the help we can get."

Homer fell to his knees and begged God to save his wife and baby. He cried and sobbed as his mother and father kneeled beside him. Her parents seemed to be frozen in fear as if they couldn't believe what was happening. Then, her mother fell into a chair and began to weep. She moaned, "Oh my baby. Oh my baby girl. Please dear God, save her and our little grandbaby." All five of them continued to pray in desperation for the two they loved so much.

After about an hour or so, they heard slow footsteps coming toward them. Each looked up, with red-swollen eyes, to see the doctor. His head was down as he walked toward them. He sank into a vacant chair. He choked out the most terrible words Homer had ever heard, "We lost both of them. Abigail lost so much blood so fast her heart gave out. We had to pull out the baby. It died from lack of oxygen from her dramatic blood loss before we could get it out. I am so sorry."

The grief stricken family was given an opportunity to see Abigail and the baby. It was a baby boy. Abigail seemed to be asleep, but her face was ashen white. She was holding the baby in her arms. Each family member kissed both the baby and Abigail. Homer asked to hold the baby. The nurse gave him his little son as he rocked him while his tears dropped on the baby's face. The nurse asked if they wanted a photo of the baby. The family said yes. It would be the only photo of their first grandchild and they treasured it the rest of their lives.

The funeral was incredibly difficult for both families their close friends and the whole town. Since the town was so small, almost everyone grieved for Homer and the grandparents. The local shops hung black wreathes on their doors and they closed the shops during the funeral. Abigail was buried with her baby boy cradled in her arms. Homer left after the graveside services; he knew he couldn't take seeing the two of them lowered into the ground. After that day, Homer was a lost man. He couldn't sleep or concentrate and eventually had to quit his job. He moved to a hotel because living in their home reminded him of his tragic loss. Eventually, he returned to live with his parents.

Homer became bitter and angry with God. He didn't attend church and refused to get help. He said he wanted to feel his pain and he needed to fully grieve the loss of his family. He said that if he didn't go through the full mourning process, he would never heal. To ease his pain, he buried himself into helping Herbert with the farm. At night, he often wept until he feel asleep. Annette could hear him and she cried too. Her wonderful son was in pain and she felt his pain and suffering, too. Then, one day, she got the courage to talk to him. It was after dinner on a cold, dreary November night. The first big holiday, Thanksgiving, was a few days away. She knew that it would be a lonely and wretched time for Homer.

She saw Homer sitting on the front porch in the cold and looking out over the fir trees. They seemed to glisten in the moonlight. The rich, warm perfume of their greenness filled the air. He breathed it deeply into his lungs and wished his little son was there to share it with him. Absorbed in his thoughts, he didn't notice Annette gently move toward him. She quietly asked, "Homer. May I sit with you for a short spell?" Homer looked up and said, "Yes. I need someone beside me tonight."

She sat a few minutes then said, "Homer. How can I help you? I don't know what to do. Your pain is my pain. Moms feel their children's pain even when they become adults. We never break the bond we have with our children." Homer sighed and answered, "I think I know what you mean. I keep seeing my little boy and my wife laying in the hospital bed. I can't get it out of my mind." She took his hand and gently caressed it. It was rough and cold.

She said, "Homer. It's too cold out here. Let's move inside." He shook his head to indicate he wanted to stay outside. With a broken and devastated voice he answered, "Mom. Now I know how you felt when you lost my sister. How did you get over it? How could you go on?" She took her hand and moved his face toward hers, "You never get over the pain. There will always be a hole in your heart. I mourn for

170

her every day, but when you came along, well, I was busy loving you." He nodded as if he understood what she was saying. She continued, "Whenever I see a little girl with unruly blond hair, running around and laughing, my heart seems to stop and my chest feels tight. I feel like I have been robbed. Robbed of the joy of my little girl."

Homer dropped his head into his hands, "I don't understand why God took them away. Every morning when I wake up, I drag myself out of bed. I dread each new day because it is another day without them." He began to softly weep. She put her arm around his broad shoulders and said, "I think I know exactly how you feel. I lost my little girl, and then my beautiful daughter-in-law and my little grandson. Homer, I don't think I can lose you, too. Homer, please come back to me. Your mama needs her son and her son needs his mama."

Homer fell on her shoulder and wept as he had never wept before. That night, his tears were filled with the anguish of his incredible loss. When he finished, he felt as if he could breathe easier. That night was the first night he slept without dreaming about walking into the hospital room seeing his wife and baby laying cold and still in the hospital bed.

After that night, Homer began to slowly heal. He returned to church, but couldn't sing or play his guitar for a very long time. Then one day he picked up the guitar and started to sing. When Annette heard him, she cried. This time, they weren't tears of pain. They were tears filled with hope for final healing for her son. Homer changed as he moved from isolated grief to living in the present. He was still sad inside and yearned to be able to feel the joy he felt with Abigail. He wondered if he would ever be able to love again. He had been given a few years of incredible joy and completeness; was there to be no more? He wondered if the chance of it happening a second time was possible.

During the following years, Homer met a few women. Sadly, none captured his heart as had Abigail. He began to think he was too particular and since he wasn't getting younger, maybe he should settle for something less. Then, after a few more disappointing relationships, he dropped into a deep depression. His father decided to talk to Annette. He shared that Homer seemed different; quiet and often forgetful; not like his normal self.

Annette said she noticed Homer wasn't eating well and that he kept to himself after the work day. Both agreed either Homer was physically

sick or something was bothering him. Annette
chose to talk to her son. She knew he tried many
times to find a wife, but things hadn't worked
out. She pondered how to best talk to him?
What would be the best approach? Then, she had
an idea; maybe a change of scenery would be
good. She called his brother in California and
asked his advice. He said, "Mom. Funny that
you called me. I was just getting ready to call
Homer."

The call came the next day after Homer
finished helping his dad on the farm. His brother,
Willard, called. He lived in a small California
farming town about a few days travel south of the
family farm. Willard said a local farmer needed
someone right away to work on his harvesting
and packing-shed equipment. The farmer, he
said, was hard up for a skilled repairman. If
something wasn't done right away, he could lose
most of his crop. He said if he ordered new
machines, it would take several weeks to arrive.
Even if the crops were picked in time, the
packing shed needed extensive work, too. This
sounded great to Homer. He immediately packed
up and made the long trip, by bus, to the town
where Nina lived.

*Nina. Now God will reveal His gift to you,
someone to love, cherish, respect, protect and
provide for you, for the rest of your life.*

"We love him, because he first loved us."
1 John 4:19 (KJV)

Chapter 10

Autumn Love

Nina knew she was falling in love. For the first time in her life, Nina was experiencing something new and wonderful. She looked forward to every moment with Homer and was beginning to think that he would be part of her life, forever. Then, abruptly one day, Homer told her he would be leaving to return home. She was stunned; after all, he had mentioned the farmer wanted to hire him as his fulltime mechanic. Nina asked in shaky voice, "Homer. Why are you going home?"

He smiled and answered, "Don't worry Nina, I will be back. I have business to attend to at home before I can accept the new job. You see, my parents depend on me to keep their farm up and running. They can't afford to hire someone to repair the farm equipment and also help dad run it. If I left, they may have to shut it down." Nina gasped, "Oh no, Homer. That would be awful." Homer took her hand and said, "I need to make sure they will have the help they need, before I take this new job. Nina, will you wait for me?" She smiled, then answered, "Homer. I am not a young woman and you are the first man to court me. Well, I think that is what you have been doing, you know, courting me? Who else would I be waiting for?"

He gave her a loving look, then said, "You are the most amazing woman I have ever met." She gasped at what he said. Then she began to tremble and her legs got weak. Homer saw her emotional reaction, he pulled her close and tightly held her in his arms. Nina responded to his embrace and said, "Oh, Homer. You don't really know me. If you knew what I have done and what I was, you wouldn't be courting me or even talking to me." Nina looked into his eyes then began to cry. "Homer. I have a dark and sinful past. I am not worthy of you."

He gently cradled her face in his hands and whispered in her ear, "I will rejoice greatly in the Lord, my soul will exult in my God; For He has clothed me with garments of salvation, he has wrapped me with a robe of righteousness, as a bridegroom decks himself with a garland, and as a bride adorns herself with her jewels." She softly moaned and leaned closer into his embrace. Then, suddenly, feeling unworthy of his love for her, she tried to pull away.

He carefully took her hands and pulled her even closer and cuddled her in his strong arms. As he held her whispered in her ear, "O my dove, that art in the clefts of the rock, in the secret places of the stairs, let me see thy countenance, let me hear thy voice; for sweet is thy voice, and thy countenance is comely." He continued to speak his words of love for her, "Thy lips are like a thread of scarlet, and thy speech is comely: thy temples are like a piece of a pomegranate within thy locks." Nina put her head on his shoulder and quietly sobbed as he tried to console her.

He said, "Do you know that your name Carolina means strong? It is the perfect name for you. You are a woman who is resilient and strong because you have broken the chains of Satan that bound you. You see, everyone in town knows who you were and who you are now. I knew all about you when I came to church that first night. I love you because you love God. I love you not because you are perfect, but because your imperfectness has made you humble, caring and filled with godly love. Nina. You are a true woman of God and I love you for it."

He continued, "That first night in church, I was hoping to meet you. When Hank walked back and welcomed me, he invited me to join you and Linnie. I couldn't believe my luck. Not wanting to be too forward, I decided to sit in the back. Then I thought, if I stay in the back I won't see your face. That was when I volunteered to play my guitar and sing. I kept looking over at the two women sitting by Hank. I picked you out right away. I noticed you wouldn't directly look at me. Then, one time you smiled ever so slightly and we locked eyes. You seemed to be embarrassed and then closed your eyes and looked away. I noticed your face was peaceful and kind. I knew right away, I must get to know you. I am glad I did. Nina, you have given me a chance to love again after I thought I never would."

Hearing those words, she knew Homer was truly another of God's amazing gifts. Nina raised her head to face Homer. Her eyes were red and her cheeks were covered in salty tears. Homer showered her face with kisses. He brushed her hair from her forehead as he gently caressed it, full of love. She relaxed and fell into his arms; they were strong and steady. She said, "Homer. Where did you learn such beautiful words?" He smiled and answered, "They are from the Holy Bible; The Song of Solomon. Have you never read it?" Nina returned his smile and said, "No, but you can be sure I will read it now. God's Word always amazes me." Home asked, "You didn't answer my question. Will you wait for me?" Nina giggled, "Oh Homer. How could I refuse? What are thinking will happen when you return?" Homer answered, "You will find out when I do."

Homer left a few days later. They hugged, kissed and said the things that people in love say. Nina cried as he boarded the bus. She knew, in her heart, that when he returned he would ask her to marry him. She was certain of it. She was happy about it and she was glad her life was different. Yes, God had been following her for many years. He was carrying his gifts of love for her; free gifts of happiness and a new life, clean and bright. When she turned and walked toward God, His gifts were freely given. Yes, she was grateful she finally stopped running from God. She often wondered where she would be if she hadn't. Would she be dead or old and haggard and bitter as in her dream? One thing she knew for certain, right now her life was totally different.

When she returned home from the bus station Linnie was waiting for her and said, "Nina. Did you think that in the autumn of your life you would be a bride? I know I didn't think that I would. Me and Hank gettin' married was a surprise to me. I was in my forties and so was Hank. Being Hank's wife has been purely wonderful for me. I know you will have the same life too."

Nina, Time to prepare for your new life and for more gifts from God.

"Thou wilt shew me the path of life: in thy presence is fullness of joy; at thy right hand there are pleasures for evermore."
Psalm 16:11 (KJV)

Chapter 11

I Am With You Always

Homer didn't return for over a month. Nina began to worry that he wouldn't return. Even his weekly calls didn't ease her fretfulness. Linnie could see the pain in Nina's eyes. She prayed with her and tried to comfort her. During his absence, all of her past fears began to replay in her mind. Everyday Nina cried and expressed to Linnie that she was not worthy of Homer. After all, she often said, his parents may not want their son to marry an ex-prostitute.

Unable to sleep and concentrate, she couldn't eat and lost weight. Seeing the sudden change in her appearance, Linnie suggested Nina visit the doctor. Nina responded, "I know what's wrong with me and I don't need a doctor. I need Homer. I need him here beside me." Linnie answered, "Give him time. Don't smother him with your fretting. He is a good man and his word is good enough."

The day Homer started home to Nina, he called her. Nina was resting in her little house. Red, her new dog and protector had been sleeping on the floor next to her. He became her guardian after Gator died. One evening, he showed up at her little house. Nina heard a dog whimpering, looked out her screen door and saw a big-red dog looking at her. Immediately, he stole her heart and they became inseparable. His incredible hearing and keen sense of smell told him Linnie was close by. Red was alert and waiting at the door to welcome Linnie. Nina saw Red move to the door. She sat up and looked toward the door, but saw no one. She moaned and said, "Oh Red. I wish it was Homer you thought was at the door." Downhearted and disappointed, she lay down in bed then heard a knock. Nina said, "Homer, is that you?"

Linnie answered, "It's me, Linnie." Nina slowly got out of bed and walked toward the door. As she did she patted Red on the head. Red wagged his tail and gave Linnie a welcoming bark. Linnie found the screen unlocked and walked inside. Nina said, "I don't lock it because Red wouldn't let a stranger in the house. I thought I could never replace Gator, but Red has perfectly filled the job." Linnie said, "Wake up sleepy head. Homer called and is waiting to hear your voice. Hank is keeping him company until you get there."

Nina's eyes widened at the mention of Homer's name. She rushed past Linnie and Red and ran out the door. When she reached Linnie's house, she pushed open the front door and hurried to the phone. Hank looked up and said, "Here she is now. I'll let you two lovebirds talk." He handed her the phone as she excitedly said, "Homer, are you coming back to me?" He was surprised at her greeting, he answered, "Calm down Nina. Sure I am coming back. I never left you."

Hearing his voice, Nina began to cry, then sob. Her voice was quivering as she replied, "Homer. Oh, Homer. I can't wait to see you." He answered trying to quiet her crying, "Nina. Don't cry. Can you meet me at the bus station in two days?" She breathlessly responded, "Can I? Absolutely. I will be there waiting for you. I have missed you so much." Homer's voice was calm as he assured her he loved her and couldn't wait to see her. They talked a few more minutes before saying goodbye. When Nina hung up the phone, her tears were dry and she was wearing a huge, glorious smile.

Nina was a different person for the next two days. Hank said she was prancing around like a new colt. Nina would laugh and hug Linnie and Hank as she waltzed around in response to her happiness. She was in love and the man she loved would be home, very soon. It seemed as if everyone who was around her
187

noticed her dramatic change. The customers and her co-workers at the variety store noticed how much she perked up. Her new found energy and happy personality made her workday enjoyable for everyone.

She wondered if that was what her life would be like from now on. Was that what it meant to be in love; to wake up each day with joy in your heart? Was that what the scriptures were trying to teach her? Her current Bible study was the book of Psalm. There was a particular verse about joy (Psalm 15:11) she re-read many times during those two days of waiting. "Thou wilt shew me the path of life: in thy presence is fullness of joy; at thy right hand there are pleasures for evermore." The verse gave her renewed faith that God was working many wonderful miracles in her life.

While Nina waited, Homer rode the bus down the big central valley. Most of the landscape was farming or dairies. It wasn't very interesting scenery, so he turned his thoughts to a problem he was trying to solve. He was apprehensive about what he would tell her. He kept trying to find the right words but couldn't. So, he gave up and prayed for help. He prayed she would understand and accept his dilemma.

The problem was that his parents really needed his help during the winter holidays. They couldn't do the backbreaking holiday setup and also sell the trees by themselves. They asked him to come home during late November and all of December. Since no crops were harvested during November and December, he wasn't worried about asking his boss for the time off. Homer was concerned how Nina would react and if it would change her mind about marrying him. He had observed how she seemed to fall apart when she thought they would be separated. He was worried she may choose to stay single.

The two days passed and his bus finally pulled into the small bus station. He saw Nina waiting. She spied him and enthusiastically waived to him. Homer's stomach began to tighten. He said a short prayer before he left the bus so his face wouldn't show his concern. As soon as he stepped off the bus, Nina ran to him and he pulled her close. She had been crying. He said, "Why are you crying?" Nina answered, "I don't know. I guess it is a woman thing. You know we cry when we are sad and we cry when we are happy." He laughed and began to relax. He thought that maybe he should wait until later to bring up the subject about which he was worried. Homer held her hand as he picked up his one suitcase. Relieved that the man she loved was home, Nina tightly grasped his arm as the two of them walked to Hank and Linnie's.

When they arrived, Hank and Linnie were sitting on their front porch. Red was there waiting for Nina to return. As soon as he sensed they were near, he stood and barked to welcome them. Nina ran to him and scratched his ears, then scratched his back. Red made his funny sound, deep in his throat to tell Nina he liked having his back scratched. Hank stood up and hugged Homer. He said, "Me and Linnie are pretty happy you made it back safe. We know you had a long ride. We prayed for a good trip. I reckon it was safe enough cause you don't look ruffled." Homer replied, "Yes sir. It was smooth and quiet. I got a fine rest. How is everything here? Anything interesting happen while I was gone?"

Hank replied, "Well. We lost our preacher. He had to go back home and take over his dad's church. His dad had a heart attack and needed his son to keep the church going. We miss him and hope we can find a new preacher. We got quite a few that is gonna' come talk." Homer put his hand on his chin and said, "If I was a preacher, I might be interested." As soon as the words left his mouth, he regretted saying it. He knew it was impossible. How could anyone keep a church going when the preacher was gone November and December of every year.

Nina spoke, "I know you would be wonderful. Of course, I am prejudiced." Linnie responded, "We all agree but I bet you are starved for a good home-cooked meal. Let's go inside and get something to eat. I got a roast in the oven with potatoes and carrots. Nina made a cake; your favorite German Chocolate." Homer laughingly said, "You mean, my girl can cook?" Nina furrowed her brow and pointed her finger at him. She teasingly replied, "Yes. Your girl has been learning to cook and she is doing quite well, thank you."

The meal was great, the conversation was lively and the evening ended on a happy note. After dinner, Nina walked Homer to Willard's house. Willard and his wife, Denise, asked her in to visit. She didn't stay long, she had to go to bed early because she was working the next day. After the short visit, Homer walked her to the gate and kissed her goodnight. Nina said, "Oh, Homer. Your neighbors think we are a couple of silly teenagers out here necking in the front yard."

He answered, "You make me feel like a teenager." She giggled and waived as she walked away. Homer yelled out, "Go straight home. The sun is beginning to set. I don't want you dallying along the way and walking in the dark." As Nina walked backwards she yelled, "You are sure bossy these days." He laughed and waived to her as she turned the corner to walk a few blocks home.

Once back inside his brothers' house, Homer asked Willard if he could talk to him in private. He shared his concern with Willard. Willard didn't respond immediately to what Homer told him. Homer asked, "What would you do? Would you tell her right away?" Willard answered, "You need to tell her up front. Don't wait. If you don't, she may think you are the type who hides things from her. Whatever her answer is, you will know you were forthright with her. Although, I doubt if it will make much difference to her. I think she will be happy staying here while you are gone. She will be content being close to her friends and church family."

He continued, "I have been married for twenty years. One thing I learned was never to hide anything from my wife. Hiding the truth caused me more misery than what I had to tell her." Homer sighed, a deep and worried sigh. He said, "Well, I guess that is the answer I need. I will talk to Nina tomorrow when she returns from work. I just don't know how she will react. She is so emotional and I worry about her getting depressed. You know she depends upon me so much. I don't know if I can make her feel safe when I am not around. She has been through so much I want her to know she can always depend on me, even if I am hundreds of miles away."

The next afternoon, when Nina got off work, Homer was waiting for her outside the store. Nina had quit her cocktail waitress job and was managing the local five and dime store. It was a variety store with a food counter with tall stools for the customers. Locals frequented the store where they could get a piece of pecan pie, bowl of ice cream, or soft drink and sandwich. They had a good amount of customers because they served the fresh pies from the local bakery.

As with most small towns, all left over food was given to the local homeless center that was a soup kitchen for the poor. It was run by kind volunteers and it was never empty. Most of the people who ate there were migrant farmworker families. Homer saw Nina walking out of the store with one of the migrant farmworker families. They were laughing and talking. Homer was pleased to see his beautiful Nina laughing; oh how deeply he loved her.

As soon as Nina was outside the store, the two hugged and shared a quick kiss. They walked holding hands and making small talk.

Nina told Homer, "There was a time when I couldn't walk down this street. I was an outcast and not welcome. Things are different now. I can shop in town and visit with some of the women customers and not be ashamed. You know, God did a real miracle with me. I am not the same person." Homer squeezed her hand, he turned to face her and they stopped walking.

He said, "Nina. You are truly an amazing woman. You have endured hardship and tragedy so terrible most people would have caved in. I am proud to be standing here with you. I don't want to be with anyone else but you. Not now, not ever." Nina touched his cheek and sweetly answered, "You are another free gift from God. I didn't ask for you and I didn't expect you. God knew I needed you in my life. I am the one who is blessed." Homer said, "Let's get something to eat. How about the new Mexican food place?"

As they ate, Homer talked about his time with his parents. Nina listened intently, she wanted to learn as much as she could about his family. She did know a few things about Homer. He was a widower. His wife and child died during childbirth. He said he vowed he would never marry again. Many times he shared that losing a child and spouse at the same time was too much pain for anyone to carry. Although he never said

194

it, she thought that one reason he came to the small town was to get away from his misery and loneliness.

He told her that each time people at his hometown brought up the subject of his loss, it was as if he was reliving the nightmare. Nina took heed to what he said and vowed to never to ask him anything about it. She didn't want to cause Homer to relive those sad years. Deep in her soul, she believed he would never be totally healed of his tragic loss. Although, she was thrilled that he seemed to be happy and at peace when they were together. In her heart, her desire was to bring him the love he deserved. As they visited at the restaurant, the topic of marriage came up.

Homer said, "Nina. I haven't formally asked you to marry me. Before I do, I have something to ask you." Nina looked at him, puzzled by what he said. She paused and then started to respond. Homer put his fingers over her mouth. He said, "Don't answer. Let me explain something to you." He took a deep breath and started, "My parents need me to help with their business. They can't make a go of it without me. Now, don't get upset. I can live here most of the year, but when the November and December holidays come up, I must go home to help them."

He paused, waiting to see how she was taking in what he said. He noticed her facial expression didn't change.

He continued, "I know how close you are to Linnie and Hank. I don't want to take you away from them. I also know how hard it is on you to be away from me. I will be going home to help my parents almost two months each year. What do you think? Will that be a problem and will you be ok while I am gone?" Nina got a surprised look on her face, she smiled and said, "Gosh. I thought you were going to tell me something terrible. Maybe that you were sick or couldn't marry me. Homer, I don't mind, not one bit. As a matter of fact, I would like to go with you. You know, I am a strong and capable woman. I can do my share of hard work."

Homer grinned then began to laugh. Nina joined in as they sat at the table holding hands and laughing. Other customers looked their way and smiled at the couple so deeply in love. After a few moments, Homer released her hand, kneeled beside her and said, "Nina. Would you give me the pleasure of being my beautiful bride?" Nina tried to answer, but paused for a second. Some of the women customers stood up and yelled, "Yes! Yes! Please marry the man!"

Nina gasped and answered, "Well, Homer. There is your answer. Of course I will marry you. You know, I am learning you are a worrywart. You had nothing to be concerned about. I would have said yes, no matter what problems we might be facing." Homer pulled a small box from a pocket in his jacket. He put her engagement ring on her finger. As Nina looked at the beautiful ring the restaurant broke out in applause.

They were married in Linnie's church where Homer first met Nina. It was a small and intimate wedding. The church ladies did an amazing job of decorating, cooking and making certain Nina's wedding was perfect. Hank was the best man and Linnie was her maid of honor. Nina wore a yellow dress made of dotted Swiss. It had white lace around the neck with a full skirt and fitted waist. She wore a white hat with yellow flowers. Homer was handsome in a black suit, tie and slacks. He even bought new, shiny-black shoes to wear in place of his comfortable work boots. The church pews had white and yellow bows tied on the end. There were tall stands of white and yellow flowers that Homer's parents ordered from the local flower shop. Nina thought everything was perfect.

Even Red was there, sitting in the back row watching his Nina. Nina turned and looked at Red when the ceremony ended and called him to her. He walked slowly up the aisle and lay down by her feet. Nina leaned over and scratched his back. Red made his funny noise, deep in his throat, as if to tell her how much he enjoyed it. Red was to watch over Nina for several more years. Although, he wasn't buried in the yard behind Linnie's house; he would be buried many miles away.

After the simple ceremony, there were sandwiches, sweet tea and lemonade, and potato salad and coleslaw. One of the church ladies made the wedding cake. It was three layers; all white and decorated with white flowers with green leaves. On the top were two plastic figurines; a groom and bride. After the ceremony, the two changed clothes and prepared to leave for their honeymoon. Not owning a car, the newlyweds rode a bus to the coast. It was the first time Nina had ever seen the Pacific Ocean. The few days they were there was full of new and wonderful experiences for Nina.

She commented to Homer that the beach was nothing like she had dreamed it would be. She was surprised to find the ocean water was cold and dark. She had imagined it would be warm and clear enough to see the fish in it. She also was surprised that the weather was damp and foggy. During their walks, she saw sea lions, elephant seals and surprisingly a school of dolphins in the distance. Homer spied a whale in the deep ocean and helped Nina find it. He told her that they were married when whales migrated to the warmer seas of the Pacific Ocean.

They dined in the small huts that lined the harbor and watched the activity in the bay. They enjoyed watching the fishing boats come into port to unload their catch. They marveled at the seagulls and other birds that dove and fought to grab the bones and other fish waste that was thrown into the water. Rowdy sea lions could be heard barking and diving with stolen fish scraps. She mused that nothing was wasted and that all of God's creatures shared in the day's catch. When nightfall came, the pier was quiet and the ocean water seemed to be still. As they sat on the pier, they were content to gaze out over the ocean and breath the cool-salty air.

During those days, Nina fell in love with the Pacific coast. When it was time to return home, she asked Homer, "Will you bring me back here? I love this place. It is peaceful and beautiful. Let's promise to come here every year on our anniversary." Homer responded, "Nina. I will take you anyplace you want to go to." Nina smiled and patted his hand, she said, "How did I ever deserve you? I never thought I would be so happy; not ever. I can't imagine being any happier than I am right now. I love you so much, Mr. Homer Judkin."

When they returned to Nina's little house, it didn't take long to discover it was too small for two adults. Homer mentioned to his boss that they were looking for something a little bigger. They were in luck; he had a small house for rent, not far from Linnie and Hank. It had two bedrooms, a cozy kitchen with white cabinets and a laundry room next to it. There was a tiny breakfast nook and a living room with a big front window. A full bathroom with shower and bathtub was at the end of the only hallway. Nina was pleased to find that the hallway was lined with linen closets. Homer was happy with the one-car garage even though they didn't own a vehicle. Homer would be able to work on farming equipment and not worry about getting wet when it rained or cold during the foggy days.

In the backyard, Homer built Red a big dog house. Red stayed in the backyard when Nina wasn't home. When Nina was home, Red could be found lying at her feet. Red was her dog and Nina was who he loved and protected. The three of them lived in the small house most of the year. During the holidays they traveled to Homer's Christmas tree farm. Hank and Linnie took care of Red while they were gone. Things went smoothly for several years and Nina truly enjoyed working on the farm.

One day she asked Homer, "Do you think we can move up here? I know Hank and Linnie would enjoy the quiet countryside and the beautiful trees." Homer answered, "Someday. Yes, of course someday. My mom and dad aren't getting any younger. There will be a time when they will need me to take over the farm. My brother doesn't want it. He has a good teaching job and his wife doesn't like the solitude of farm life." It wasn't long until Homer had to make that decision.

Some months later, about three o'clock in the early morning their phone rang. Homer instinctively knew it was something about his parents. He answered, "Hello. Is this dad?" A female voice answered. "No, Homer. It's your mom. We lost dad a few hours ago." Homer gasped, he asked, "Mom. I will be right there. Is anyone with you?" She softly answered, "Yes, two church friends are here." Homer said, "Thank the Lord for your church family. I will come right away. I will be catching the bus tomorrow. I think I should arrive within two days." Annette told him that two days was good because she wasn't alone and she had a lot of help.

She said she talked to Willard and he would drive up right away. She mentioned that he may wish to ride with Willard. Homer answered, "Mom. There isn't room for me and Nina and his family. It will be easier if Nina and I ride the bus." They talked a little more, then ended the call. Homer immediately dialed Willard. The two brothers agreed it was best for Homer and Nina to take the bus. Their plan was that they would arrive within one day of each other.

Homer immediately got bus tickets and Nina hurriedly packed. They asked Hank if he and Linnie would keep Red while they were gone. They happily agreed. The day they left, Linnie gave them a packed lunch of sandwiches and fruit with her freshly-made homemade cookies and a thermos of hot coffee. She said that sometimes the places to eat along the away weren't good. She said it was best to take at least one packed lunch. After accepting the lunch, they said their thanks and gave hugs all around. Red was there to see Nina off; he had a sad look on his face when the bus drove off.

This was the first time Red was at the bus station when they left. All the other times, they left Red at home with her friends. Hank had to keep his leash tight; Red struggled to chase after the bus. His Nina was leaving him and he didn't know if or when he would see her again. Hank told Nina that when she called two days later to say they made it safe and sound, Red whined when he heard her voice. The rest of the day Red was unsettled and roamed around looking for her. Hank said he found an old robe of Nina's in the extra bedroom and lay it on the floor for Red. Red curled up on it and went sound asleep.

Moving North

It was cold and wet the day of Herbert's funeral. Everyone at the graveside service huddled under their umbrellas to protect them from the icy rain. As the rain poured, thunder was heard in the distance. As soon as the graveside service ended, those in attendance hastened to their cars. Everyone quickly drove to the dry, warm church. It was the home church of Homer's family. Once there, Homer introduced Nina to other family members and close friends. This was the first time Nina had been surrounded such by a large group of people. She was timid at first, but eventually warmed up to them. All were friendly and seemed delighted to meet the woman who stole Homer's heart. Although, many had been doubtful that he would marry again, they immediately understood why Homer loved Nina. They saw how much she loved him. Instinctively they knew she was the perfect person to help him heal from his tragic loss.

A few days after the funeral, Homer and Willard were busy helping their mom with various family documents. She was concerned about keeping the family farm up and running. Homer spent time comforting her and informing her he and Nina would be thrilled to take it over. That was good news. Annette had been worried that Nina wouldn't want to move so far from her close friends. Knowing this, Homer designed a plan to bring Hank and Linnie to the farm. He knew he would need them; most of all he knew Nina needed them.

Eventually, the tasks were completed and Homer and Nina were ready to travel home. As they were making plans to ride the bus, Annette asked Homer, "Son. I think dad would want you to have his truck. It is paid for and I know you could use it. He loved his old truck but it finally got unsafe for him to drive. So, he bought a new one. He enjoyed driving it. He would be happy knowing his son was sitting in the driver's seat. Please accept it from dad." Homer was surprised and stammered, unable to answer for a few seconds.

After the shock of what she said subsided, he answered, "Mom. Why don't you sell it. You can get a good sum for it. I know you could use the money." His mother answered, firmly and directly, "Homer, stop it. Dad took good care of me with his life insurance. It was your dad who was the last person to drive it. I wouldn't hear of anyone else but his own flesh and blood sitting at the wheel." That was how Homer and Nina finally got an automobile. They were thrilled to drive home in their own vehicle.

The trip home was pleasant and for once they didn't sleep in a bus seat. They stayed overnight at nice, clean motels and ate in good restaurants. On the way home, Nina said, "Homer. We are so blessed. God knows our needs before we do and he fills them every time." Homer answered, "I agree. We both have been blessed. Somehow, I think that now I can tell you about what happened to my wife and baby."

He paused for a second, took a deep breath and said, "After my wife and baby died, I had to sell everything to pay the hospital and the funeral bills. I was left with absolutely nothing. Mom and dad wanted me to move in with them. At first, I objected and flatly refused. I changed my mind after I spent a few months in a rundown hotel. It was nice to move home. Mom made great meals, did my laundry and I loved working with dad."

Nina didn't interrupt or comment. This was the first time Homer had opened up about his life after he lost his wife and baby. She moved closer to him and put her arm around his shoulder as he drove. Homer continued to talk, "I needed those years with my parents. It helped me heal. For much too long, I was lost and my life was empty. Almost everything I loved and valued was gone. You know, childbirth is supposed to be a wonderful event. I wasn't ready or even expecting the tragedy that happened. When we went to the hospital my wife seemed fine. After a few hours of waiting, the doctor left her and came to talk to me. I could tell from his eyes that things weren't right."

He stopped, swallowed and pushed back tears. "The doctor said, the baby was not in the right position. We can't turn it around and I don't know if we can operate. Also, your wife has started to hemorrhage. My heart almost stopped beating; I think I began to panic." Homer continued. "The doctor asked me to call all our parents. I asked the doctor if I could see her. He said, 'Just for a few minutes. We are getting ready to sedate her for surgery.' I almost didn't recognize her; she was so white and couldn't open her eyes to speak to me. My heart sank as I left the room to call everyone. Those were the hardest phone calls I ever had to make. They all rushed to the hospital; we prayed and cried and tried to encourage each other. It wasn't long until the doctor came in to talk to us; he said both of them were gone."

Homer pulled the truck to the shoulder of the road, turned off the engine and hit the steering wheel with the palm of his hand. Trying to gain control of his emotions, he said, "Nina. This is so hard. It isn't fair to keep you in the dark. I want to ask you something. I hope you don't want children. I couldn't stand knowing I could lose you too." Nina answered, "Homer. I don't think I can have children cause I am too old. I have already gone through the menopause. I went through it early. The doctor said it was because I had lived through a lot of abuse. Even if I wanted children, I can't get pregnant."

Homer, relaxed and lovingly said, "If I was ever to have children, it would be with you. But, I can't go through it again. I guess the good Lord knew what he was doing when He put us together." Nina answered, "Maybe the Good

Lord has kids waiting for a mom and dad. We would be good parents. I know we would love them as much as natural parents." He took Nina in his arms and they both cried for a few minutes. Their tears blended as they mourned for Homer's loss. During those few minutes, the two became much more close. To Nina, the closeness of comforting her husband felt good. It was a new and fulfilling sensation and she was grateful to experience it.

When they arrived home, their first stop was at Hank and Linnie's. Both were surprised to see a new truck stop in front of their house. Red was standing at the front door; his strong senses knew Nina was near. When Homer and Nina stepped out of the truck, Hank opened the screen door and Red rushed to Nina. She rubbed his ears then leaned forward to scratch his back. Red made his happy sounds to tell Nina he liked what she was doing. The rest of the day was spent visiting and then the two men took a ride in the truck. During their absence, Linnie asked Nina, "How was it? Was his family nice to you?" Nina answered, "Linnie. His family is nice and are real kind people, just as much as he is. You would feel right at home being around them." Her answer pleased Linnie; she had been worried Nina would be greeted by a cold and judgmental family.

For the next few months, Homer made plans to move Nina and Red up north with his mother. He wanted to get things completed as soon as possible. If they waited too long the holidays would be upon them and the full winter weather would be too harsh to travel. During those days, he had asked Hank and Linnie if they would relocate and live with them on the farm. At first, both refused. As the two learned more and discovered there was already a house for them, they began to reconsider. Linnie didn't try to sell her house, she knew the new preacher needed a place for he and his wife and his mother-in-law. Linnie's house was perfect. She also left her second-hand furniture. The preacher said it was too expensive to ship their furniture and he was happy with what was already in the house.

It seemed as if everything worked out perfectly; the farmhouse they were to move into was totally furnished. It had been Homer's grandmother's home. The furniture was old, sturdy and quite beautiful. It was covered in plastic tarps since her death; a few years earlier. Her china, cooking utensils, and more were still there. Homer's mother sent photos and Linnie fell in love with it. It was a perfect house for she and Hank. Annette assured everyone it would be ready for them to move in as soon as they

209

arrived. She said the church ladies were doing a thorough cleaning to get it ready for them.

The plan was that Hank and Linnie would travel by bus and Red would ride with Nina and Homer. Since they would live with his mom, they took only what would fit into the back of the truck. The family house had four bedrooms and two were on the second floor with a full bathroom. The two of them would have privacy and his mother would have hers too, downstairs. It was a perfect plan; only God could design such a plan. The decision was to sell as much of Homer and Nina's things as possible. The small amount of money from the sale of their furniture provided plenty for their trip.

Within a short time, all were ready to travel. Nina was excited about the move, although she regretted not being able to go to the coast on their anniversary. She shyly mentioned it to Homer. He replied, "Nina. My home is not far from the northern coast. It is exactly like the place we spent our honeymoon. I will make certain we go there for every anniversary." This soothed Nina's heart and she thanked God for her wonderful husband. Homer kept his promise. Every anniversary was celebrated at the coast. They gathered many wonderful memories each anniversary and Nina cherished them with all her heart. Although, before they left to move to live with Homer's mother, there was one more thing Nina needed to do.

The Final Farewell

Nina wanted to go to the junkyard to tell her brothers goodbye. She told Homer about her brothers and how they died and where they were entombed. He said he would take her. Hank and Linnie would go, too. They would all ride in Homer's truck. Red and Hank would sit in the back of the truck while Homer, Linnie and Nina would ride in the front. Sensing a potential danger or something that would upset or hurt Nina, he asked the new preacher to meet them at the dump. The day came and the ride was quiet and solemn.

Nina's heart was heavy and her hands were shaking. Linnie hugged her and with one hand she firmly grasped Nina's trembling hands. Linnie knew this would be a traumatic event for her; she had shared the details of Nina's brother's death with Homer. He was surprised he hadn't heard the full story before. He told Linnie that Nina needed God, at that time, more than ever before. He said that the demons that controlled her brothers could be waiting to harm Nina.

It was a good thing the preacher was there. When Homer pulled up with the truck, all of them felt a heavy and oppressive spirit hovering over them. Nina's shaking took a bad turn. She began to cry and sob with uncontrolled dread. Homer was hesitant to let her get out of the truck. He said, "Nina. You don't have to do this. Please tell me if you can't, I will take you home." Between sobs, Nina spoke with a strong voice, "I got to do it. I just got to. I will never be able to close the door and put it behind me. I got to face them. If I don't, I will always be haunted by them."

Homer said, "Linnie, you and I need to pray for protection from Satan's demons. When we get out, I am going to ask the preacher to help us pray. This is serious; Satan always wants to win. He won't give in, he will fight Nina with all his strength" They lay hands on Nina and prayed for protection for her and everyone there. Then they guardedly let her step out of the truck. As soon as Nina's foot hit the ground, Red was at her side. His teeth were bared and he was making a deep and threatening growl. The hair on his back was standing up, his ears were upright and his tail was down and between his legs. He moved in front of Nina and tried to push her back into the truck.

Nina touched his head and said, "Red. I must do this. I know you can tell there are evil spirits here. We got to trust God to keep all of us safe." Red looked up at Nina and whined, then he took an attack stance and glared at the pile of junk before them. Just then, the preacher stepped forward. He said, "I can feel evilness here. We should turn around and leave." Nina refused. Oddly, she was no longer shaking or crying. She stood erect and tall and was ready to face whatever Satan prepared for her. The small group interlaced their arms and walked slowly toward the mangled mass; black and unidentifiable.

It didn't look like a vehicle; it resembled the face of a devil with two black horns standing on top of a head. To the side of the head, it looked like two hands with long claws that appeared to reach outward. As Nina walked, to her it felt as if each step sounded like an explosion. The preacher walked ahead of them, praying and reading the Bible. Red had moved beside him and was crawling on his belly as he slowly crept forward. All of them stopped within a few feet of the black mass. The preacher took a bottle of holy water and tried to sprinkle it on the black mass. Something flung it from his hand and it broke on the ground.

He stopped, backed up a few steps and fell to his knees. He threw his arms in the air and screamed, "Satan. You have no power here. We are children of God. The power and majesty of God surrounds us. Satan, I present to you the Living Word of God." Then, he held up the Bible and presented it to the black mass. An incredibly wicked sound poured out of the blackened-mangled mass. It began to shake. Yes, it was shaking and the ground began to move and everyone almost lost their balance. The five of them huddled together in an attempt to stay standing. Red was ready, he flew forward and was in a full fight with something invisible.

The five watched in amazement as Red flung an unseen enemy into the air. Within seconds, Red was standing over his evil opponent and was viciously growling at it. His head was frozen as if he was glaring at something wicked. Then, the ground quit moving. It was still and quiet. Red stepped off whatever he was holding, turned and ran to Nina. He slumped down and lay by her feet; panting from his combat. Nina fell to her knees and hugged and kissed Red. She was crying uncontrollably; it was a good cry, one of relief. Then, a loud crash filled the air. The huge blackened-mangled mass fell apart and was crumpled on the ground. It hit the ground so hard that dirt and gravel flew through the air.

Miraculously, none of the five were hit with the debris or even received a minor cut.

The ugly mass was unrecognizable. It looked like a pile of tiny pieces of black rock. Whatever had been holding the evil sarcophagus together was gone. As it left, it fell apart. The preacher broke the silence, "Satan's demons escaped from the wreckage. Where they went, we don't know. What we do know is that Red fought with one of them and Red won. I believe Red was given the power and strength of the Archangel Michael who wages war with Satan's evil angels. Let us give thanks to our Father in Heaven for His protection." The preacher, Homer, Nina, Hank and Linnie and even Red all knelt that day on clean ground. It was unsoiled because God prevented Satan's shattered black mass from landing on His Holy Ground.

As they knelt and prayed, the preacher read Revelation 12:7-9: "And there was war in heaven: Michael and his angels fought against the dragon; and the dragon fought and his angels, And prevailed not; neither was their place found any more in heaven. And the great dragon was cast out, that old serpent, called the Devil, and Satan, which deceiveth the whole world: he was cast out into the earth, and his angels were cast out with him." After he finished, everyone stood, including Red as they turned their backs and walked away from the worthless rubble. Yes, it was rubble and no longer held any power to wield Satan's fury on God's creation.

As everyone headed home, Nina said, "Homer, please drive down Old Telegraph Road. There is one more thing I need to do." He gave her a puzzled look, then turned the truck around and headed toward it. Once there, Nina asked again, "Please stop at this intersection. This is where everything started." Homer obliged, but had no idea what she was referring to. She explained, "You see, Homer. When I was running from God and living for Satan, I came here one night with a young man. There was a big group of local teens and other partiers. Hard liquor and beer were consumed in great amount and most of them were pretty drunk. I didn't drink a lot, just a few sips of coke with Sloe Gin in it. Let's get out of the truck and I will tell you the whole story."

They stepped out of the truck and stood looking at the old oak tree; it was standing like a sentinel in front of them. Nina began to recall that night during the early 1960s. She said, "There was a bunch of us standing around our cars; about a quarter mile up there. We were dancing, laughing and having a good time. Then, someone yelled over a bullhorn that the race was starting. You see, this road was where the local kids raced to see who had the meanest and fastest car. That night, one local teen raced against two men from the city. It was a terrible night that spiraled me into deep and awful sin." She took a deep breath, grabbed Linnie's hand and said, "This isn't easy for me to share."

Linnie responded, "Ornella wasn't here. She was in the city with a friend. She called me when you were brought home. She said you were in a bad way and she wasn't sure if you would live through the night. Ornella begged the doctor to come and examine you. He couldn't, too many others had been injured. So, I came and did what I could. I hope you have forgiven me for giving you the shot of valium and the hard liquor while you was sickly." Nina looked at Linnie, "It wasn't your fault I got addicted to valium and other drugs. It was my fault because I had been following Satan. I believed his lies that only he had what I needed to calm my spirit. I don't blame you. I probably would have died without your help."

Nina continued her story as she gripped Linnie's hand much tighter. "The men from the city had a car with a lot of power. They also had other plans that night. The rumors were that they were going rough up all of us after the race. We didn't know that two other cars were close by hiding their gang member friends. They had knives, brass knuckles, chains and all sorts of weapons. The men in the purple car had a trunk

217

with jars full of gasoline; they were going to throw them at us after the race ended." She took a deep breath and said, "Even though they didn't, what happened next was terrible."

In a somber voice she continued, "The cars took off and sped toward us. Their car was too fast for the local kid. He never had a chance. When their car got close to the old oak tree, it became airborne. None of us had seen a car fly off the pavement. We were in shock and thought it would fly right into us. Instead, it hit the old oak tree. When it did, their car burst into flames and it sounded like a bomb exploded. The kids sitting in the tree were thrown in the air and blown apart. I was hit with something on my chest. When I put my hand on it, it felt hot and sticky. I looked down and saw a finger with a ring on it. I guess I fainted because the next thing I remember was Linnie talking to me; about a day or two later."

Linnie began to weep and Homer stood watching Nina with a look of amazement. Nina said, "This is the first time I have talked about that night. I can do it because God has given me peace about it. All these years, I have kept it bound inside my heart and soul. Right now, I feel that I have been freed of my fear. That old oak tree has taken two hard hits that should have flattened it or killed it. Instead, it still stands. You know, I think it saved a lot of lives that

night and the night my brothers hit it. I believe it
should never be cut down; there should be a
plaque or something on it that says, 'Here stands
the town protector. It saved the lives of our
residents.' Someone should write the dates on the
plaque so that it will be a part of the town's
history.'"

When she finished, Linnie hugged her and
thanked her for forgiving her. Homer seemed to
be astonished at the story. In a few minutes he
gathered his senses and said, "Oh Nina. I didn't
know you suffered so terribly. I thought my pain
was the worst; but, you have endured so much
more. You know, God knew we were both
suffering inside. Maybe that is why he brought
us together, because you understand my pain."
Nina looked lovingly at Homer and said, "You
are my soulmate and God found a way to bring
you to me." Homer held her close and said,
"Now we have each other and the past is behind
us. Soon, all of us will be in a new place. Now
we can start over as a family that God made."

A day or so afterward, Homer, Nina,
Linnie, Hank and Red headed north. They were
to embark on a new life, in a new place and with
renewed energy and strength. They lived
together for many happy years on the farm.
During those years, God continued to bless them.
The farm prospered and Nina and Homer did
have children. Not children of their own blood,

they adopted a brother and sister who had lost both their parents. In the autumn of their life they discovered a different type of love; the love of raising children in a Godly home. It was exactly what God knew they needed. They agreed it was His plan and His plan is always perfect.

Those years on the farm Hank was a great help to Homer. Hank enjoyed the outdoors and relished in the fruits of his labor. He would stand looking at the evergreen trees and marvel at the perfection of God's creation. As well, Linnie and Annette became close friends. Linnie learned to make homemade jams and candies. She also enjoyed helping Annette with her small quilting business. Homer found Nina to be a joyous helpmate with the farm and the children. They both adored parenthood in the late years of their life. It was something they never expected; but quietly wanted.

After all, God knows what we need and He desires to bless us with His gifts. He is always ready to fulfill our needs and desires of the heart. He was able to do so when Nina turned around and acknowledged that God was waiting for her. At that time, she had no idea of the many gifts He had prepared for her. The same is true for all of us; if we would just turn around and accept and love God. It is that simple.

Nina. God has lavished you with love;
but there is much more to come.

Nina, Your Mother is Near

Nina, the first time I held you, my baby so sweet:
My heart filled with love, my life was complete.

Too soon, we were parted and no longer near;
Too long, I searched for your face to appear.

One day as I walked through a field full green;
I saw you in the distance and fell to my knees.

I cried out to God for my chance to be near;
The daughter I lost who was running in fear.

You smiled as you noticed your mother so close;
"It is I", I said, "Your mother, not a ghost."

Oh daughter of mine, I have returned to retrieve;
The daughter I lost who is now near to me.

Come daughter, day is falling.
Come daughter, mother is calling.
Come daughter, I'm here by your side;
Come daughter, forever I will abide.

Written by: Zelma Frankhouser

*"Teaching them to observe all things whatsoever
I have commanded you: and, lo, I am with you
always, [even] unto the end of the world. Amen."*
Matthew 28:20 (KJV)

NINA'S FINAL JOURNEY

I am over eighty years old with hair, gray and thin and my once strong body is frail and bent. Today is no different than any other day as I reminisce about my life. I sit on the porch and slowly rock back in forth in the chair Homer bought me. The smooth motion of the chair relaxes me as I marvel at the beauty of our evergreen trees. Their lush branches are heavy with needles. The clean freshness of pine essence fills the air with their redolent fragrance. As I breathe the heavenly perfume, I think about how much my Homer loved me and I marvel at how God brought us together. The love I had with Homer was totally unexpected and one that filled me with awe each time I looked at him. Many years ago, when he took me too his family farm I discovered a new understanding of God and how much he loved me. The man I loved was truly God's gifts to me and this farm was His incredibly beautiful creation. It is during the stillness of the evening hour that fills my soul with heavenly delight of living on the farm.

The beauty of this farm takes my breath away each time I gaze upon it. Nothing can rival the rich emerald color of the trees, especially when the golden rays of the sun caress its branches.

They seem to glisten in the sunlight as they exhale their balm. I am renewed each time I deeply breathe the caress of their clean perfume. It fills my soul with wonderful memories of the over thirty years spent on the farm.

As a young girl, I thought that I would never spend the end of my life surrounded by such inconceivable beauty. My beginning years were tainted with misery, pain and fear. God freed me of my sinful past and my agonizing childhood memories. It will always be a mystery to me why God chose to lavish me with such unbelievable happiness and love. I guess I will never understand the depth of His love.

I am a child of God and one who is blessed and filled with the Holy Spirit. I cannot count how many times I have been healed and encouraged by it. Truly, I have been showered with goodness so lavish that nothing on Earth can rival it. Yes, my dear and wonderful Holy Spirit, you will always remain a mystery to me. The first time I felt its embrace was when Linnie held me in her arms and prayed for me. That was the beginning of my total transformation. That was many years ago; now I am old and sit in my rocking chair and watch the day turn to evening.

I remember when my Homer bought me this chair. It was my sixtieth birthday. He said he loved seeing me sit in it as he walked home from work. He said when he came out of the trees, the first thing he saw was me. He could see peace and happiness in my eyes. Each evening, as he walked toward me, he would waive and smile. He always stopped to kiss me before going inside to wash before dinner. Yes, living on the farm brought me amazing joy and peace.

My heart aches because I miss my Homer; he died four years ago. Now, my days are long and empty because I have lost so many that I loved. My lifelong friends, Hank and Linnie grew old with hair, white and unruly. As Linnie aged, she kept her hair long and pulled in a tight bun. I always smiled at the stray hairs that surrounded her face. When a breeze came up, they would dance as if waiving at something invisible. I would say, "Your hair is wavy today cause it's waiving at the sky." She would laugh and brush them back in place with her hand and say, "Oh Nina. At least I have unruly hair. Poor Hank is almost totally bald. Just think, when we met he had a full head of hair."

Linnie was the first to pass on to heaven. She became ill with emphysema; most likely from her previous years of smoking. I can still clearly remember the day she left us. Hank said he was getting her a cup of strong coffee then he heard a thud. He turned to see Linnie crumpled over on the kitchen table. When he walked into our house, I could tell from the look on his face that Linnie was gone. The doctor said she died right away and didn't suffer.

Hank followed a few years later. One cold and misty morning, Homer went to get him so they could walk together to start work. That was his usual routine; to stop by Hank's and they would walk to the trees together. Homer found Hank sitting in his favorite chair; his hands dropped to his side. Homer said he looked as if he was sleeping. Then, we lost Homer's mother one year later. She awoke one morning unable to get out of her bed. The doctor said she had suffered a grave stroke. She was taken to the hospital and died within a week. Now, it is just me and our two grown children and their little ones.

I guess I shouldn't be lonely, I got my kids and grand babies to keep me company. But it just isn't the same, I have a deep emptiness in my heart for all that are no longer here with me. I especially miss the times me and Homer spent our anniversaries on the Pacific Coast. Every year, he kept his promise to take me there on our anniversary. He would stop his farm work and would say, "It is time I take my bride to the coast because she loves it so much and because I love her even more." Those times we were together at the coast are treasured memories. I guess I shouldn't cry about them, but I can't stop the tears from flowing when I remember.

These days, my grand babies always ask why I cry so much. I tell them I cry because I have happy memories and because I love them. Of course, at their young age they don't understand. Our two adopted children take good care of me and have kept the farm up and running and successful. I never asked them to take over the farm. They chose to do it because they said they loved it. Well, they have done a great work with it. It is still beautiful and people come from far and wide to purchase their trees for Christmas.

My goodness, I think I must be dreaming. I see something beautiful in the sky. It looks like a rainbow, but with hundreds of stunning colors. I think it is moving toward me. Yes, it is slowly swirling and flowing all around me. Oh my, it has a wonderful aroma; something like lavender, bergamot, roses and orange blossoms mixed together. It is embracing me with its gentleness and delightful perfume. It must be my imagination; I think my eyes must be playing

229

games with me. Well now I really must be dreaming because I see something walking towards me. No, it isn't a person, it is an animal. No, not one but two dogs. One looks just like my faithful Gator and the other resembles Red.

Oh my, they are scrambling up the porch steps. They both lay at my feet and are very friendly. I hope they aren't lost. I think I will scratch behind their ears just as did with my dogs. What? I can hear them groan as if to say they enjoy it. I wonder if I should keep them; I would enjoy their company. Oh, now they are standing and looking out at the stand of trees. What do they see? Yes, they see someone walking toward me. It looks like my mother. It can't be cause my mama died when I was a little girl. Mama has been gone a very long time. Dear heavenly father, I believe it is my mama.

The Journey Home

As Nina visits with her mother, another person emerges from the stand of evergreen trees. Nina looks up and recognizes the woman. Yes, she knows who it is; it is Ornella her friend who died over fifty years ago. Behind Ornella is Linnie and Hank and they look like they did when she first met them. She again thinks that she is dreaming. She turns to see the three of them looking at her; she smiles and they return her smile. Her mama walks over to the porch swing and sits next to Nina and the two dogs. Nina turns to the side and takes her hand. Her mother kisses her cheek, the same as she did when Nina was little.

Nina touches her cheek then gazes lovingly at the group that has joined her on the porch. They are all sitting on the porch, talking softly as they visit. She is no longer lonely and sad. Then, she looks to her side, and Homer's mother is there. She says to Nina, "Would all of you please join us for supper? It isn't anything fancy. Homer and dad will be home soon for supper. Let's fry a chicken and make mashed potatoes and corn. Do you want to make a German chocolate cake? You know, it is Homer's favorite."

Nina stands, and answers, "Of course mom. Homer and dad will be here by dark and they will need a good home-cooked meal. They need their strength to keep this farm going." Nina stands and the two women hold hands as they walk to the kitchen to prepare supper. Nina says, "You know, mom. I never thought my life would be so wonderful. God surely must love me, something grand. "

Nina. Your Earthly journey has ended and your Heavenly journey has just begun. It is your time to live in God's eternal love and to never to be afraid or alone, again.

Nina, you have reached you destiny.

Other Books by Zelma

MY BELOVED
THE HEAVENLY BRIDE

The most powerful of human emotions is love. We seek it, long for it and we cannot live without it. It is an overpowering emotion that cannot be measured, defined, proven or even adequately described. Often, the one that is loved is called My Beloved. The Biblical Song of Songs also described the one that is loved as My Beloved. It was written thousands of years ago and is filled with songs of longing, deep desire and declarations of love. Song of Songs contains a phrase that means, 'I am his and my beloved is mine". It is an incredibly beautiful phrase that describes our relationship with our Creator God for He calls us His Bride - His Beloved. This study is designed to bring those who love God into a new and deeper relationship as His Beloved. It contains historical information about the Ancient Hebrew wedding, lecture notes with breakout activities, a weekly study and a year-long personal reflection journal. It is full of

235

Hebrew words that will bring deeper meaning regarding God's love for His creation.

THE OTHER SIDE OF THE CROSS SERIES

If you enjoy books by Francine Rivers, you will enjoy the series *The Other Side of the Cross.* All books in this series are fiction but based on real-life experiences and are written to encourage those struggling with life to reach out to God for help.

Yeshua (Jesus Christ) gave His life on the Cross for our sins. Those who find themselves trapped in Satan's snare of lies, deception, pain and hopelessness have hope in Yeshua.

Yeshua shed His blood on one side of the Cross so that we need not shed our blood for our sins. Therefore, the other side of the Cross which is clean represents the cleansing of our sins that was completed on the other side of the cross. It is done; accepting Yeshua's gift of salvation and His forgiveness for our sin is all that is needed.

BEAUTIFUL FEET

Beautiful Feet is a book that reveals the life of a fictitious person who does battle with Satan. As she struggles to be free of her mental torment, she loses control of her life. As such, the reader may find parts of the book upsetting; specifically those sections that document her pain. These sections are critical to understanding the depth of her despair and her overwhelming need for Christ.

Beautiful Feet is based upon Romans 10:15, Isaiah 52:7 and Nahum 1:15. "And how can they preach unless they are sent? As it is written, 'How beautiful are the feet of those who bring good news'" (Romans 10:15 NIV). *Beautiful Feet* reveals the splendor of lives forever changed through Christ Jesus our Lord and Savior.

Beautiful Feet also records a compilation of my memories when I was twelve years old and I attended a small, country church that provided my first opportunity to learn about Jesus Christ.

ELIZABETH

My name is *Elizabeth* and I lived in a small town when I was four-years old. My first remembrances of childhood began on Lanai Street. Lanai is a terrace or veranda, a place of beauty, relaxation, and pleasure. In some ways Lanai Street could be described as a place of beauty; but deep within the walls of some of the homes evil dwelt; an evil spirit that stole the breath and life of little children.

I lived in a small house with my momma and daddy. I was a precocious child that caused my family a lot of grief. Even though I made a lot of silly childhood mistakes I was always disciplined in love. I loved my momma and daddy. Daddy worked hard in the fields and momma stayed home to take care of me. I stopped talking one day and the doctor didn't know what was wrong.

I knew why I wouldn't talk but I was afraid to tell. You see, the Swamp Woman was trying to steal my breath, so I just quit talking all together. I finally told her to leave me alone and she did. Once she left I started to sing. The lady at school who was in charge of everything heard me sing and she thought I was real good. When I got older, I went to New York to learn to sing and to get a good education.

NINA

My name is Nina, it rhymes with China. This is my story. I lived it, I hated it, and I ran from it. One day I turned around and realized I had been running in the wrong direction; I was running toward Satan not knowing God was always beside me.

My story begins during the 1960s, but the first chapter sets up the entire book during the 1860s. You see, a hundred-year old tree played a large part in freeing me of my tormentors; my evil brothers. The tree was strong, tall and resilient. It watched over the area to keep it safe. Many bandits were hung from its branches and more than once it stopped really bad people from harming the residents of my town.

I was terribly abused as a young girl by my evil brothers. I escaped but they found me even when I lived 3,000 miles from them. Don't think the entire book is about my struggles; God was faithful to bring me an incredibly wonderful love in the autumn of my life – a man who deeply and faithfully loved and protected me.

THE RED DUST OF OKLAHOMA SERIES

If you enjoy books by Laura Ingles Wilder's *Little House on the Prairie,* or other authors such as Janet Oke, you will love reading the series – The Red Dust of Oklahoma. All books are fiction but are based on real-life experiences.

Take a trip back in time when America was struggling with two simultaneous nationwide tragedies: the 1930s Great American Plains Drought and the Stock Market Crash.

This series describes how families in eastern Oklahoma survived by keeping their faith in God and practicing strong family values.

SEEKING HIDDEN TREASURE
COMING LATE 2020
A LOVE STORY DURING THE 1940S

Five years passed and I (Margarita) am a teenager. I attend edmy best friend's birthday party. When I saw Millie's fiancé, I got a funny feeling. I began to blush. That night, I had a strange dream that I was to be his bride. I felt ashamed that I would dream such a thing.

A few days later, Millie ran to me crying. Her fiancé was to leave for a full year to work in Texas with his brother. She was distraught and almost inconsolable. I held her and hugged her and told her not to worry. I tried to comfort her by telling her that the year would go by fast and as soon as he returned they would be married. I was wrong.

Millie would not see her fiancé the next year; he wouldn't return for two years. When he returned he was different, no longer a young boy. He discovered Millie had become impatient during his long absence; she was engaged to someone else. I began to think my dream was a foretelling of my future.

THE TREASURE HIDDEN WITHIN

Margarita's family faces new challenges to their family. This book is filled with scriptures, prayers, and the enduring faith of Margarita's family as they experience the TREASURE hidden within.

The TREASURE appears to be the answer to surviving the ongoing drought; but, it actually is something much deeper. As the reader, you will discover how the scriptures of the Bible deliver hope and the amazing miracle of surviving difficult times. This book is not about religion or one denomination. It is about loving, trusting, calling upon God, and building a family tradition of faith in God.

"Unto thee, O LORD, do I lift up my soul.
O my God, I trust in thee: let me not be ashamed, let not mine enemies triumph over me.
Yea, let none that wait on thee be ashamed: let them be ashamed which transgress without cause.
Shew me thy ways, O LORD; teach me thy paths.
Lead me in thy truth, and teach me: for thou art the God of my salvation; on thee do I wait all the day.
Remember, O LORD, thy tender mercies and thy loving-kindness; for they have been ever of old."
(Psalm 25:1-6 KJV)

243

THE SECRET IN
GRANDMA'S SUITCASE

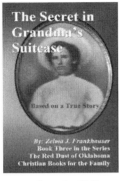

What is the secret in grandma's suitcase? Is it family secrets or is it something else? Margarita discovers it through her close friendship with her grandma. Find out about the secret and how it changed not only Margarita's life but also grandma's life.

The Callison family immigrated to America many years ago. They were of Irish descent and originated from North Omagh County, Ireland. My mother, Margaret Allen (Alan) Frazier Robison, helped take care of her Grandma Hattie when she became frail. Mother loved her very much and enjoyed every minute with her.

The authors' great-grandma Hattie was barely five feet tall and her husband was Grandpa Callison. She kept candy and oranges in a suitcase in her room. She invited her grandchildren, one by one, to share the treats with her so she could enjoy talking to them. Much of this book is based upon Grandma Hattie and my mother when she was a young, precocious girl growing up on a farm in eastern Oklahoma.

THE MYSTERY OF THE PAINTED WAGON

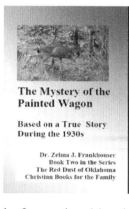

The Mystery of the
Painted Wagon

Based on a True Story
During the 1930s

Dr. Zelma J. Frankhouser
Book Two in the Series
The Red Dust of Oklahoma
Christian Books for the Family

Read Book Two in the series of fictional stories for the young reader, *The Mystery of the Painted Wagon* to your children, grandchildren, and Sunday school class. The main character, Margarita Eileen turns seven-years old and is ready to start school. The summer before school begins her Uncle McCauley brings a green and yellow gypsy wagon to her farm. Why he left the wagon with her family and where he got the wagon is a mystery. Woven throughout *The Mystery of the Painted Wagon* are lessons about truth, faith, and trust.

She and her cousin (who is paralyzed from polio) spend many fun days on the family farm. You will enjoy reliving the simple life on a farm in eastern Oklahoma when there were no phones or television and when kids played using their imaginations as they freely roamed the countryside. That summer, Margarita Eileen gives her heart to Christ and learns the meaning of Proverbs 30:33, "For as churning the milk produces butter, and as twisting the nose produces blood, so stirring up anger produces strife" (NIV).

245

GRASSHOPPER IN THE WINDOW

The first book by Dr. Frankhouser, is **Book One** of a series of fictional stories for the young reader. It is written from the eyes of a six-year-old girl who loves living on a farm with her family in eastern Oklahoma.

It is a delightful story that introduces the young reader to family life during our nation's great depression, circa 1930. Their farm produces most of the family food, income, and is the setting for all her social interaction, and spiritual training.

The story recounts how her devotion to prayer and faith in God carries her through many challenges and heart-breaking experiences. Those who teach Bible studies, home school their children, or mentor at-risk children may find this series helpful as supplemental teaching material. Book appendices provide opportunities for discussion and Bible research.

BE FORGIVEN

*"I acknowledged my sin unto thee, and mine
iniquity have I not hid. I said, I will confess my
transgressions unto the LORD: and thou
forgavest the iniquity of my sin. "*
(Psalm 32:5 KJV)

There is eternal hope and blessings for those
who act to receive Yeshua (Jesus) and who act to
ask for forgiveness. This simple act will result in
joy and liberty from the chains with which we are
shackled by sin. It is done; there is no other debt
to pay.

Be Blessed and Rejoice

*"Blessed is he whose transgression is forgiven,
whose sin is covered. Blessed is the man whom
the
LORD imputeth not iniquity. "*
(Psalm 32: 1-2 KJV)

*"Be glad in the LORD, and rejoice, ye righteous;
and shout for joy, all ye that are upright in heart. "*
(Psalm 32:11 KJV)

THE AUTHOR

 I was born in Oklahoma. At the age of four, my family moved to California. There were six of us in my family. My family worked in the fields and the first few months in California we lived in a tent and then a one-room house. As a very young child, it was too dangerous for me in the fields. I stayed in Oklahoma with my grandmother, Cora, during harvest season. When I was old enough I joined my family in the fields, I continued to help them until the age of thirty. At that time, I took a job in education. I worked in education for twenty years and retired early to take care of my aging mother. During those years, I returned to school and completed my bachelor, master and doctorate degrees. After obtaining my degrees I became an adjunct university professor and also taught at an adult school. After my mother passed away, I started writing small books about my mother and our family in Oklahoma. Recently, I began to write Christian suspense novels. Nina is the third book I have written in this genre.I pray you will enjoy reading my books and you will be encouraged to seek your dreams. Anything is possible with God.

Zelma Jean Robison-Frankhouser

INDEX

---

[i] c https://manlinesskit.com/hair-tonic/. Pomade hair tonic, In the 1960s, hair tonics and pomades all but dropped from most men's daily regime with the introduction of styling gel and mousse. Men have, since their inception, always been the primary users of hair tonics. These are unique from most hair care because they are almost always in liquid form (pomade is sometimes considered a tonic in some respects).

When your father or grandfather went to the barber, often hair tonics were called massage lotion or friction lotion. This is largely because they were used to give the customer a stimulating scalp massage. It served as a double whammy for hair health as the blood was stimulated to react with the hair follicles and the tonic infused the hair and scalp with moisture for conditioning purposes.

Just as barbers have done for years, hair tonic is intended to be massaged deep into the hair and onto the scalp. This allows the tonic to interact with every part of the hair and scalp.

[ii] DAVID M. HERSZENHORN. July 2, 1995. Wolfman Jack, Raspy Voice Of the Radio, Is Dead at 57.
Wolfman Jack, the rock-and-roll disk jockey whose unmistakable raspy voice and on-the-air howls brought him something of a cult following as one of America's best-known radio personalities, died yesterday at his

home in Belvidere, N.C. He was 57. He was born Robert Smith in Brooklyn on Jan. 21, 1938, and for a couple of years in 1960 and 1961 he was Daddy Jules on WTID in Norfolk, Va., But he cascaded to fame as Wolfman Jack, a faceless hero on the AM airwaves and a pioneer of the peculiar genre called border radio, because it was broadcast from just over the border in Mexico. He was among a group of border disk jockeys in the early 1960's with names like Hound Dog and Huggy Boy, and he had his name legally changed.

From 1963 to 1966, Wolfman Jack howled and growled at night on XERF-AM in Via Cuna Cohuilla, Mexico. In 1966 he moved to XERB, where he spun the latest rock tunes from a small studio in the sleepy resort town of Rosarito, overlooking the Pacific Ocean, 15 miles south of the United States border. The station pumped out at 250,000 watts, five times the legal limit for American stations at the time, and was heard across most of the country. In the studio, he was every bit as crazy as he sounded, with his face contorting, his eyes bulging and his hands waving wildly.

It was not until he played himself in the 1973 film "American Graffiti" that fans could match the voice with a face. And they were not disappointed. The Wolfman looked the part, with bushy eyebrows, sideburns, a mustache and a devil's goatee.

In 1962 he worked at KCIJ, a country station in Shreveport, La., where he went by the name Big Smith With the Records. Byron Laursen, a New Jersey writer and co-author of Wolfman Jack's autobiography, said that Wolfman Jack also worked in an interracial nightclub called The Tub, which was housed in an old Quonset hut,

251

and served as host of a weekly interracial dance party for teen-agers.

iii Online. 2017. https://www.allmusic.com/artist/bobby-lewis-mn0000071409/biography. Biography by Bruce Eder. Bobby Lewis is one of those talented performers whose recognition is confined to a single monster hit, "Tossin' and Turnin'." Released in early 1961, the single rode the charts for 23 weeks, eventually hitting the number one spot on both the pop and R&B charts. Lewis had other hits, including a Top Ten follow-up with "One Track Mind," and had been working for years before that, yet the one song came to be his signature.

Bobby Lewis was raised in an orphanage, and ran away from his foster home at age 14. He worked carnivals, and eventually joined the Leo Hines Orchestra in Indianapolis as a singer. He worked small clubs and theaters during the '50s, and cut "Mumbles Blues" for the Spotlight label early in that decade, passed through the Mercury Records roster, and briefly hooked up with Nat Tarnopol, who also managed Jackie Wilson.

In late 1960, while appearing at the Apollo Theater in New York, Lewis stopped at the offices of Beltone Records, a small independent outfit in Manhattan, and was prevailed upon to record a song written by another artist on the Apollo bill, Ritchie Adams, called "Tossin' and Turnin'." The single was issued at the end of 1960, and lightning struck in 1961 -- sales of the record were so strong that for the only time in its history, Beltone issued an accompanying album by Lewis. None of his subsequent records sold remotely as well as the three

252

million copies of "Tossin' and Turnin'," and by the end of 1962, Lewis seemed to have run out his string; in 1963, Beltone itself went belly-up. Lewis later had limited success ("Stark Raving Mad") on ABC-Paramount, and was soon after consigned to rock & roll history, somewhat unfairly, as a one-hit wonder.

[iv] Online. 2017. www.songfacts.com. In the liner notes of Dion's box set King Of The New York Streets, he wrote: "It came about by partying in a schoolyard. We were jamming, hitting tops of boxes. I gave everyone parts like the horn parts we'd hear in the Apollo Theater and it became a jam that we kept up for 45 minutes. I came up with all kinds of stuff. But when I actually wrote the song and brought it into the studio to record it, well, her name wasn't actually Sue. It was about, you know, some girl who loved to be worshiped but as soon as you want a commitment and express your love for her, she's gone. So the song was a reaction to that kind of woman."

v Online. 2017. www.songfacts.com. K-Doe's real name: Ernest Kador. Born in 1936, he remained a popular singer and radio personality in New Orleans until his death in 2001. While best known as a singer, K-Doe was also an accomplished drummer.

The song plays on the stereotype of the meddling mother-in-law who feels the man who married her daughter isn't good enough for her. Most songs of this nature would be labeled "novelty" records, but K-Doe's sincere delivery kept that tag off the song in most publications.

This song was written by Allen Toussaint, who was Ernie K-Doe's producer. Toussaint came up with the song when he was playing piano in his family's living room, messing around with bits of a song he had heard from the Gospel group the Harmonizing Four. Trying to think up lyrics, he came up with the title and quickly fabricated the story about a guy who is put through hell by his mother-in-law.

vi By Terence McArdle October 24, 2016, Washington Post, "Take Good Care of My Baby" (1961) by writers Carole King and Gerry Goffin, Mr. Vee was a Fargo, N.D., teenager and bandleader when he got his first big break replacing the rock star Buddy Holly, who had died in a plane crash in 1959 on the way to a dance near Mr. Vee's home town. Mr. Vee modeled his nasal vocal style on Holly's and, through a long string of hit songs that explored unrequited love, cultivated the persona of a cheerful underdog.

vii www.songfacts.com, This was written by the husband and wife songwriting team of Gerry Goffin and Carole King. It's a benignly sexual song with the singer wondering what will happen the day after an encounter with her man. It met with some resistance from radio stations, but not enough to stop it from becoming a huge hit, selling over a million copies. Shirelles lead singer Shirley Alston initially disliked the song, dismissing it as "too Country and Western" for the 4-girl group from Passaic, New Jersey. Their producer Luther Dixon convinced her they could do it in their style, and asked King and Goffin if they could add strings and turned it into an up tempo song, which they did.

viii www.songfacts.com, Richard Rodgers and Lorenz Hart began writing this for the 1933 movie musical Hollywood Party, but it was cut from the film. The following year, it was used in Manhattan Melodrama - starring Clark Gable, William Powell and Myrna Loy - where it was performed by Shirley Ross in a nightclub scene. The song was originally called "The Bad in Every Man," befitting the story of Gable's kind-hearted criminal, but was rejected by MGM until it was re-worked as "Blue Moon."

Producer Stu Phillips was ordered by his boss not to waste time on the Marcels and to spend his days devoted to a different artist at Colpix Records. But he didn't say anything about his nights. Phillips waited until everyone else had gone home and sneaked the band into the studio for a secret session. They recorded this at the last minute when they recorded three songs and needed a fourth. When one of the members said he knew "Blue Moon," Phillips told him to teach the song to the rest of the group in an hour, then they'd record it.

The Marcels recorded this in two takes. A promotion man asked and got a copy of the finished tape, which found its way to legendary DJ Murray The K. He promoted it as an "exclusive" and played it 26 times on one show.

ix www.songfacts.com, This was featured in the 1961 Elvis movie *Blue Hawaii*. It was written by the songwriter George Weiss, who claimed that neither the movie producers nor Elvis' associates liked the

255

song demo, but Elvis insisted on recording this song for the movie. Weiss, who died in 2010 at age 89, was a military bandleader in World War II. *Can't Help Falling in Love with You* was written by Hugo Peretti; Luigi Creatore; George David Weiss.

This was Elvis' most popular and famous "love song," but it was not sung to his love interest in *Blue Hawaii* - It was sung to his grandmother on the occasion of her birthday. Elvis presented her with a music box, which she opened and it played the song, which Elvis then sang along with.

The soundtrack to *Blue Hawaii* hit #1 on the US charts in the fall of 1961 and remained there for 20 weeks in a row, a record that wasn't broken until 1977 by Fleetwood Mac's landmark album *Rumours*.

The melody is based on a French song called "Plaisir D'Amour," which was penned in 1784 by a German with an Italian name, Jean-Paul Egide-Martini.

Made in the USA
Columbia, SC
23 August 2022